Under the Red Flag

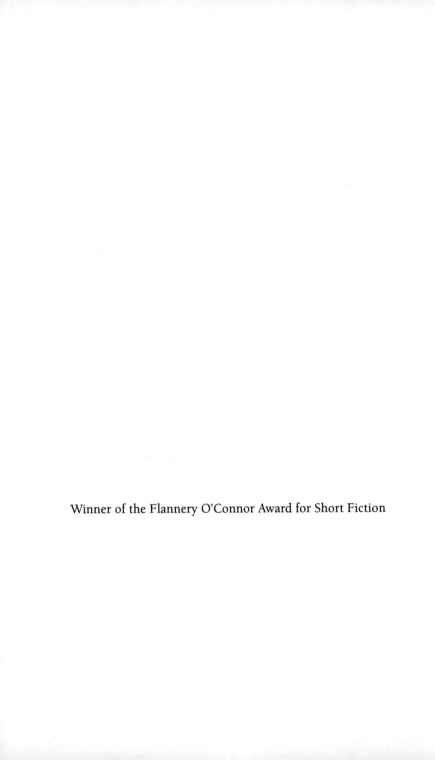

Winner of the Flannery O'Connor Award for Short Fiction

■ Under the Red Flag

1997

STORIES BY HA JIN

The University of Georgia Press ■ Athens and London

Published by the University of Georgia Press
Athens, Georgia 30602
© 1997 by Ha Jin
All rights reserved
Designed by Erin Kirk New
Set in 10 on 14 Berkeley Old Style Medium
Printed and bound by Maple-Vail Book Manufacturing Group

The paper in this book meets the guidelines for
permanence and durability of the Committee on
Production Guidelines for Book Longevity of the
Council on Library Resources.

Printed in the United States of America

01 00 99 98 97 C 5 4 3 2 1

Library of Congress Cataloging in Publication Data

Jin, Ha, 1956–
Under the red flag : stories / by Ha Jin.
p. cm.
Contents: In broad daylight—Man to be—Sovereignty—Winds and
clouds over a funeral—The richest man—New arrival—Emperor—
Fortune—Taking a husband—Again the spring breeze blew—
Resurrection—A decade.
ISBN 0-8203-1939-2 (alk. paper)
1. China—Social life and customs—Fiction. I. Title.
PS3560.I6U53   1997
813'.54—dc21   97-12235

British Library Cataloging in Publication Data available

FOR JENIFER KASDON

■ Acknowledgments

"In Broad Daylight" first appeared in the *Kenyon Review* and was winner of the *Kenyon Review* Prize for Fiction (1993) as well as the Pushcart Prize (1995). It was reprinted in *Norton Introduction to Fiction*, *Norton Introduction to Literature*, and *Into the Widening World: International Coming-of-Age Stories*, ed. John Loughery (Persea Books). "Emperor" was also first published in the *Kenyon Review*. "Man to Be" originally appeared in *TriQuarterly* under a slightly different title and was winner of the Pushcart Prize (1997). "Winds and Clouds over a Funeral" was first published in the *Indiana Review*, "The Richest Man" in the *North American Review*, "New Arrival" in the *Chicago Review*, "Fortune" in the *International Quarterly*, "Resurrection" in the *Atlantic Monthly*, and "A Decade" in *Cicada*.

■ Contents

✓ In Broad Daylight 1

✓ Man to Be 17

✓ Sovereignty 31

Winds and Clouds over a Funeral 44

The Richest Man 68

New Arrival 77

Emperor 96

Fortune 114

Taking a Husband 132

Again, the Spring Breeze Blew 154

Resurrection 169

A Decade 197

Under the Red Flag

■ In Broad Daylight

While I was eating corn cake and jellyfish at lunch, our gate was thrown open and Bare Hips hopped in. His large wooden pistol was stuck partly inside the waist of his blue shorts. "White Cat," he called me by my nickname, "hurry, let's go. They caught Old Whore at her home. They're going to take her through the streets this afternoon."

"Really?" I put down my bowl, which was almost empty, and rushed to the inner room for my undershirt and sandals. "I'll be back in a second."

"Bare Hips, did you say they'll parade Mu Ying today?" I heard Grandma ask in her husky voice.

"Yes, all the kids on our street have left for her house. I came to tell White Cat." He paused. "Hey, White Cat, hurry up!"

"Coming," I cried, still looking for my sandals.

"Good, good!" Grandma said to Bare Hips, while flapping at flies with her large palm-leaf fan. "They should burn the bitch on Heaven Lamp like they did in the old days."

"Come, let's go," Bare Hips said to me the moment I was back. He turned to the door; I picked up my wooden scimitar and followed him.

"Put on your shoes, dear." Grandma stretched out her fan to stop me.

"No time for that, Grandma. I've got to be quick, or I'll miss something and won't be able to tell you the whole story when I get back."

We dashed into the street while Grandma was shouting behind us, "Come back. Take the rubber shoes with you."

We charged toward Mu Ying's home on Eternal Way, waving our weapons above our heads. Grandma was crippled and never came out of our small yard. That was why I had to tell her about what was going on outside. But she knew Mu Ying well, just as all the old women in our town knew Mu well and hated her. Whenever they heard she had a man in her home again, these women would say, "This time they ought to burn Old Whore on Heaven Lamp."

What they referred to was the old way of punishing an adulteress. Though they had lived in the New China for almost two decades, some ancient notions still stuck in their heads. Grandma told me about many of the executions in the old days that she had seen with her own eyes. Officials used to have the criminals of adultery executed in two different ways. They beheaded the man. He was tied to a stake on the platform at the marketplace. At the first blare of horns, a masked headsman ascended the platform holding a broad ax before his chest; at the second blare of horns, the headsman approached the criminal and raised the ax over his head; at the third blare of horns, the head was lopped off and fell to the ground. If the man's family members were waiting beneath the platform, his head would be picked up to be buried with his body; if no family member was nearby, dogs would carry the head away and chase each other around until they ate up the flesh and returned for the body.

Unlike the man, the woman involved was executed on Heaven Lamp. She was hung naked upside down above a wood fire whose flames could barely touch her scalp, and two men flogged away at her with whips made of bulls' penises. Meanwhile she screamed for help and the whole town could hear her. Since the fire merely scorched her head, it took at least half a day for her to stop shrieking and a day and a night to die completely. People used to believe that the way of punishment was justified by heaven, so the fire was called Heaven Lamp. But that was an old custom; nobody believed they would burn Mu Ying that way.

Mu's home, a small granite house with cement tiles built a year before, was next to East Wind Inn on the northern side of Eternal Way. When we entered that street, Bare Hips and I couldn't help looking around tremulously, because that area was the territory of the children living there. Two of the fiercest boys, who would kill without thinking twice, ruled that part of town. Whenever a boy from another street wandered into Eternal Way, they would capture him and beat him up. Of course we did the same thing; if we caught one of them in our territory, we would at least confiscate whatever he had with him: grasshopper cages, slingshots, bottle caps, marbles, cartridge cases, and so on. We would also make him call every one of us "Father" or "Grandfather." But today hundreds of children and grown-ups were pouring into Eternal Way; two dozen urchins on that street surely couldn't hold their ground. Besides, they had already adopted a truce, since they were more eager to see the Red Guards drag Mu Ying out of her den.

When we arrived, Mu was being brought out through a large crowd at the front gate. Inside her yard there were three rows of colorful washing hung on iron wires, and there was also a grape trellis. Seven or eight children were in there, plucking off grapes and eating them. Two Red Guards held Mu Ying by the arms, and the other Red Guards, about twenty of them, followed behind. They were all from Dalian City and wore homemade army uniforms. God knew how they came to know there was a bad woman in our town. Though people hated Mu and called her names, no one would rough her up. These Red Guards were strangers, so they wouldn't mind doing it.

Surprisingly, Mu looked rather calm; she neither protested nor said a word. The two Red Guards let go of her arms, and she followed them quietly into West Street. We all moved with them. Some children ran several paces ahead to look back at her.

Mu wore a sky-blue dress, which made her different from the other women who were always in jackets and pants suitable for honest work. In fact, even we small boys could tell that she was really handsome, perhaps the best looking woman of her age in town. Though in her fifties, she didn't have a single gray hair; she was a little plump, but because of her long legs and arms she appeared rather queenly. While most of the women had sallow faces, hers looked white and healthy like fresh milk.

Skipping in front of the crowd, Bare Hips turned around and cried out at her, "Shameless Old Whore!"

She glanced at him, her round eyes flashing; the mole beside her left nostril grew darker. Grandma had assured me that Mu's mole was not a beauty-mole but a tear-mole. This meant her life would be soaked in tears.

We knew where we were going, to White Mansion, which was our classroom building, the only two-story house in town. As we came to the end of West Street, a short man ran out from a street corner, panting for breath and holding a sickle. He was Meng Su, Mu Ying's husband, who sold bean jelly in summer and sugarcoated haws in winter at the marketplace. He paused in front of the large crowd, as though having forgotten why he had rushed over. He turned his head around to look back; there was nobody behind him. After a short moment he moved close, rather carefully.

"Please let her go," he begged. "Comrade Red Guards, it's all my fault. Please let her go." He put the sickle under his arm and held his hands together before his chest.

"Get out of the way!" commanded a tall young man, who must have been the leader.

"Please don't take her away. It's my fault. I haven't disciplined her well. Please give her a chance to be a new person. I promise, she won't do it again."

The crowd stopped to circle about. "What's your class status?" a square-faced young woman asked in a sharp voice.

"Poor Peasant," Meng said, his small eyes tearful and his cupped ears twitching a little. "Please let her go, sister. Have mercy on us! I'm kneeling down to you if you let her go." Before he was able to fall on his knees, two young men held him back. Tears were rolling down his dark fleshy cheeks, and his gray head began waving about. The sickle was taken away from him.

"Shut up," the tall leader yelled and slapped him across the face. "She's a snake. We traveled seventy kilometers to come here to wipe out poisonous snakes and worms. If you don't stop interfering, we'll parade you with her. Do you want to join her?"

Silence. Meng covered his face with his large hands as though feeling dizzy.

A man in the crowd said aloud, "If you can share the bed with her, why can't you share the street?"

Many of the grown-ups laughed. "Take him, take him too," someone told the Red Guards. Meng looked scared, sobbing quietly.

His wife stared at him without a word. Her teeth were clenched; a faint smile passed the corners of her mouth. Meng seemed to wince under her stare. The two Red Guards let his arms go, and he stepped aside, watching his wife and the crowd move toward the school.

People in our town had different opinions of Meng Su. Some said he was a born cuckold who didn't mind his wife's sleeping with any man as long as she could bring money home. Some believed he was a good-tempered man who had stayed with his wife mainly for their children's sake; they forgot that the three children had grown up long before and were working in big cities far away. Some thought he didn't leave his wife because he had no choice—no woman would marry such a dwarf. Grandma, for some reason, seemed to respect Meng. She told me that Mu Ying had once been raped by a group of Russian soldiers under Northern Bridge and left on the riverbank afterwards. That night her husband sneaked there and carried her back. He looked after her for a whole winter till she recovered. "Old Whore doesn't deserve that good-hearted man," Grandma would say. "She's heartless and knows only how to sell her thighs."

We entered the school's playground where about two hundred people had already gathered. "Hey, White Cat and Bare Hips," Big Shrimp called to us, waving his claws. Many boys from our street were there too. We went to join them.

The Red Guards took Mu to the front entrance of the building. Two tables had been placed between the stone lions that crouched on each side of the entrance. On one of the tables stood a tall paper hat with the big black characters on its side: "Down with Old Bitch!"

A young man in glasses raised his bony hand and started to address us. "Folks, we've gathered here today to denounce Mu Ying, who is a demon in this town."

"Down with Bourgeois Demons!" a slim woman Red Guard shouted. We raised our fists and repeated the slogan.

"Down with Old Bitch Mu Ying," a middle-aged man cried with both hands in the air. He was an active revolutionary in our commune. Again we shouted, in louder voices.

The nearsighted man went on, "First, Mu Ying must confess her crime. We must see her attitude toward her own crime. Then we'll make the punishment fit both her crime and her attitude. All right, folks?"

"Right," some voices replied from the crowd.

"Mu Ying," he turned to the criminal, "you must confess everything. It's up to you now."

She was forced to stand on a bench. Staying below the steps, we had to raise our heads to see her face.

The questioning began. "Why do you seduce men and paralyze their revolutionary will with your bourgeois poison?" the tall leader asked solemnly.

"I've never invited any man to my home, have I?" she said rather calmly. Her husband was standing at the front of the crowd, listening to her without showing any emotion, as though having lost his mind.

"Then why did they go to your house and not to others' houses?"

"They wanted to sleep with me," she said.

"Shameless!" several women hissed in the crowd.

"A true whore!"

"Scratch her!"

"Rip apart her filthy mouth!"

"Sisters," she spoke aloud. "All right, it was wrong to sleep with them. But you all know what it feels like when you want a man, don't you? Don't you once in a while have that feeling in your bones?" Contemptuously, she looked at the few withered middle-aged women standing in the front row, then closed her eyes. "Oh, you want that real man to have you in his arms and let him touch every part of your body. For that man alone you want to blossom into a woman, a real woman—"

"Take this, you Fox Spirit!" A stout young fellow struck her on the side with a fist like a sledgehammer. The heavy blow silenced her at once. She held her sides with both hands, gasping for breath.

"You're wrong, Mu Ying," Bare Hips's mother said from the front of the crowd, her forefinger pointing upward at Mu. "You have your own man, who doesn't lack an arm or a leg. It's wrong to have others' men and more wrong to pocket their money."

"I have my own man?" Mu glanced at her husband and smirked. She straightened up and said, "My man is nothing. He's no good, I mean in bed. He always comes before I feel anything."

All the adults burst out laughing. "What's that? What's so funny?" Big Shrimp asked Bare Hips.

"You didn't get it?" Bare Hips said impatiently. "You don't know anything about what happens between a man and a woman. It means that whenever she doesn't want him to come close to her he comes. Bad timing."

"It doesn't sound like that," I said.

Before we could argue, a large bottle of ink smashed on Mu's head and knocked her off the bench. Prone on the cement terrace, she broke into swearing and blubbering. "Oh, damn your ancestors! Whoever hit me will be childless!" She was rubbing her head with her left hand. "Oh Lord of Heaven, they treat their grandma like this!"

"Serves you right!"

"A cheap weasel."

"Even a knife on her throat can't stop her."

"A pig is born to eat slop!"

When they put her back up on the bench, she became another person—her shoulders covered with black stains, and a red line trickling down her left temple. The scorching sun was blazing down on her as though all the black parts on her body were about to burn up. Still moaning, she turned her eyes to the spot where her husband had been standing a few minutes before. But he was no longer there.

"Down with Old Whore!" a farmer shouted in the crowd. We all followed him in one voice. She began trembling slightly.

The tall leader said to us, "In order to get rid of her counter-revolutionary airs, first we're going to cut her hair." With a wave of his hand, he summoned the Red Guards behind him. Four men moved forward and held her down. The square-faced woman raised a large pair of scissors and thrust them into the mass of the permed hair.

"Don't, don't, please. Help, help! I'll do whatever you want me to—"

"Cut!" someone yelled.

"Shave her bald!"

The woman Red Guard applied the scissors skillfully. After four or five strokes, Mu's head looked like the tail of a molting hen. She started blubbering again, her nose running and her teeth chattering.

A breeze came and swept away the fluffy curls from the terrace and scattered them on the sandy ground. It was so hot that some people took out fans, waving them continuously. The crowd stank of sweat.

Wooooo, wooooo, woo, woo. That was the train coming from Sand County at three-thirty. It was a freight train, whose young drivers would toot the steam horn whenever they saw a young woman in a field beneath the track.

The questioning continued. "How many men have you slept with these years?" the nearsighted man asked.

"Three."

"She's lying," a woman in the crowd cried.

"I told the truth, sister." She wiped the tears from her cheeks with the back of her hand.

"Who are they?" the young man asked again. "Tell us more about them."

"An officer from the Little Dragon Mountain, and—"

"How many times did he come to your house?"

"I can't remember. Probably twenty."

"What's his name?"

"I don't know. He told me he was a big officer."

"Did you take money from him?"

"Yes."

"How much for each time?"

"Twenty yuan."

"How much altogether?"

"Probably five hundred."

"Comrades and Revolutionary Masses," the young man turned to us, "how shall we handle this parasite that sucked blood out of a revolutionary officer?"

"Quarter her with four horses!" an old woman yelled.

"Burn her on Heaven Lamp!"

"Poop on her face!" a small fat girl shouted, her hand raised like a tiny pistol with the thumb cocked up and the forefinger aimed at Mu. Some grown-ups snickered.

Then a pair of old cloth shoes, a symbol for a promiscuous woman, were passed to the front. The slim young woman took the shoes and tied them together with the laces. She climbed on a table and was about to hang the shoes around Mu's neck. Mu elbowed the woman aside and knocked the shoes to the ground. The stout young fellow picked them up and jumped twice to slap her on the cheeks with the soles. "You're so stubborn. Do you want to change yourself or not?" he asked.

"Yes, I do," she said meekly and dared not stir a bit. Meanwhile the shoes were being hung around her neck.

"Now she looks like a real whore," a woman said.

"Sing us a tune, sis," a farmer shouted.

"Comrades," the man in glasses resumed, "let us continue the denunciation." He turned to Mu and asked, "Who are the other men?"

"A farmer from Apple Village."

"How many times with him?"

"Once."

"Liar!"

"She's lying!"

"Give her one on the mouth!"

The young man raised his hands to calm the crowd down and questioned her again, "How much did you take from him?"

"Eighty yuan."

"One night?"

"Yes."

"Tell us more about it. How can you make us believe you?"

"That old fellow came to town to sell piglets. He sold a whole litter for eighty, and I got the money."

"Why did you charge him more than the officer?"

"No, I didn't. He did it four times in one night."

Some people were smiling and whispering to each other. A woman said that old man must have been a widower or never married.

"What's his name?" the young man went on.

"No idea."

"Was he rich or poor?"

"Poor."

"Comrades," the young man addressed us, "here we have a poor peasant who worked with his sow for a whole year and got only a litter of piglets. That money is the salt and oil money for his family, but this snake swallowed the money in one gulp. What shall we do with her?"

"Kill her!"

"Break her skull!"

"Beat the piss out of her!"

A few farmers began to move forward to the steps, waving their fists or rubbing their hands.

"Hold," a woman Red Guard with a huge Chairman Mao badge on her chest spoke in a commanding voice. "The Great Leader has instructed us: 'For our struggle we need words but not force.' Comrades, we can easily wipe her out with words. Force doesn't solve ideological problems." What she said restrained those enraged farmers, who remained in the crowd.

Wooo, woo, wooo, wooooooooooo, an engine screamed in the south. It was strange, because the drivers of the four o'clock train were a bunch of old men who seldom blew the horn.

"Who is the third man?" the nearsighted man continued to question Mu.

"A Red Guard."

The crowd broke into laughter. Some women asked the Red Guards to give her another bottle of ink. "Mu Ying, you're responsible for your own words," the young man said in a serious voice.

"I told you the truth."

"What's his name?"

"I don't know. He led the propaganda team that passed here last month."

"How many times did you sleep with him?"

"Once."

"How much did you make out of him?"

"None. That stingy dog wouldn't pay a fen. He said he was the worker who should be paid."

"So you were outsmarted by him?"

Some men in the crowd guffawed. Mu wiped her nose with her thumb, and at once she wore a thick mustache. "I taught him a lesson, though," she said.

"How?"

"I tweaked his ears, gave him a bloody nose, and kicked him out. I told him never to come back."

People began talking to each other. Some said she was a strong woman who knew what was hers. Some said the Red Guard was no good; if you got something you had to pay for it. A few women declared the rascal deserved such treatment.

"Dear Revolutionary Masses," the tall leader started to speak. "We all have heard the crime Mu Ying committed. She lured one of our officers and one of our poor peasants into the evil water, and she beat a Red Guard black and blue. Shall we let her go home without punishment or shall we teach her an unforgettable lesson so that she won't do it again?"

"Teach her a lesson!" some voices cried in unison.

"Then we're going to parade her through the streets."

Two Red Guards pulled Mu off the bench, and another picked up the tall hat.

"Brothers and sisters," she begged, "please let me off just this once. Don't, don't! I promise I'll correct my fault. I'll be a new person. Help! Oh help!"

It was no use resisting; within seconds the huge hat was firmly planted on her head. They also hung a big placard between the cloth shoes lying against her chest. The words on the placard read:

I am a Broken Shoe
My Crime Deserves Death

They put a gong in her hands and ordered her to strike it when she announced the words written on the inner side of the gong.

My pals and I followed the crowd, feeling rather tired. Boys from East Street were wilder; they threw stones at Mu's back. One stone struck the back of her head and blood dropped on her neck. But they were stopped immediately by the Red Guards, because a stone missed Mu and hit a man on the face.

Old people, who couldn't follow us, were standing on chairs and windowsills with pipes and towels in their hands. We were going to parade her through every street. It would take several hours to finish the whole thing, since the procession would stop for a short while at every street corner.

Bong, Mu struck the gong and declared, "I am an evil monster."

"Louder!"

Dong, bong—"I have stolen men. I stink for a thousand years."

When we were coming out of the marketplace, Squinty emerged from a narrow lane. He grasped my wrist and Bare Hips's arm and said, "Someone is dead at the train station. Come, let's go have a look." The word "dead" at once roused us. We half a dozen boys set out running to the train station.

The dead man was Meng Su. A crowd had gathered at the railroad two hundred yards east of the station house. A few men were examining the rail that was stained with blood and studded with bits of flesh. One man paced along the darker part of the rail and announced that the train had dragged Meng at least seventy feet.

Beneath the track, Meng's headless body lay in a ditch. One of his feet was missing, and the whitish shinbone stuck out several inches long. There were so many openings on his body that he looked like a large piece of fresh meat on the counter in the butcher's. Beyond him, ten paces away, a big straw hat remained on the ground. We were told that his head was under the hat.

Bare Hips and I went down the slope to see the head. Other boys dared not take a peep. We two looked at each other, asking with our eyes who should raise the straw hat. I held out my wooden scimitar and lifted the rim of the hat a little with the sword. A swarm of bluebottles charged out, droning like provoked wasps. We bent over to peek at the head. Two long teeth pierced through the upper lip. An eyeball was missing. The gray hair was no longer perceivable, covered with mud and dirt. The open mouth was filled with purplish mucus. A tiny lizard skipped, sliding away into the grass.

"Oh!" Bare Hips began vomiting. Sorghum gruel mixed with bits of string beans splashed on a yellowish boulder. "Leave it alone, White Cat."

We lingered at the station, listening to different versions of the accident. Some people said Meng had gotten drunk and dropped asleep on the track. Some said he hadn't slept at all but laughed hysterically walking in the middle of the track toward the coming train. Some said he had not drunk a drop, because he had spoken with tears in his eyes to a few persons he had run into on his way to the station. In any case, he was dead, torn to pieces.

That evening when I was coming home, I heard Mu Ying groaning in the smoky twilight. "Take me home. Oh, help me. Who can help me? Where are you? Why don't you come and carry me home?"

She was lying at the bus stop, alone.

■ Man to Be

At the Spring Festival Hao Nan was very happy, because a week ago he had been engaged to Soo Yan, one of the pretty girls in Flag Pole Village. She was tall and literate. By custom, the dowry would cost the Haos a fortune: eight silk quilts, four pairs of embroidered pillowcases, ten suits of outer clothes, five meters of woolen cloth, six pairs of leather shoes, four dozen nylon socks, a wristwatch, two thermos bottles, a sewing machine, a bicycle, a pair of hardwood chests. Yet Nan's parents were pleased by the engagement, for the Soos were a rich family in the village and Yan was the only daughter. The wedding was scheduled to take place on the Moon Day the next fall. Though the Haos didn't have much money left after the engagement feast, they were not worried. Since they had two marriageable daughters, they would be able to marry off at least one of them to get the cash for Nan's wedding.

It was the third day of the Spring Festival. Nan and four other young men were on duty at the office of the village militia. Because the educated youths from Dalian had returned home to spend the holiday season with their families in the city, the young villagers had to cover all the shifts. It was a good way of making ten workpoints—a full day's pay, so nobody complained. Besides, it was an easy job. For eight hours they didn't have to do anything except stay in the office and make one round through the village.

Outside, a few snowflakes were swirling like duck down around the red lanterns hung at every gate. The smell of gunpowder and incense lingered in the air. Firecrackers exploded now and then, mingled with the music of a Beijing opera sent out by a loudspeaker. Inside the militia's office, the five men were a little bored, though they had plenty of corn liquor, roasted sunflower seeds, and candies with which to while away the time. They had been playing the poker game called Beat the Queen. Liu Daiheng and Mu Bing wanted to stop to play chess by themselves, but the others wouldn't let them. There was no fun if only three men drew the cards, and they wanted to crown two kings and beat two queens every time.

Slowly the door opened. To their surprise, Sang Zhu's bald head emerged, and then in came his small body and bowlegs. "Hello, kk-Uncle Sang," Nan said with a clumsy smile that revealed his canine teeth.

Without answering, Sang glared at Nan, who had almost blurted out his nickname, Cuckold Sang. People called him that because his young wife, Shuling, often had affairs. It was said that she was a fox spirit and always ready to seduce a man. People thought that Sang, already in his fifties and almost twice his wife's age, must have been useless in bed. At least he didn't have sperm, or else Shuling would have given him a baby.

Sang was holding his felt hat. He looked tipsy, his baggy eyes bloodshot. "Uncle Sang," Wang Ming said, "take a seat." Without a word, Sang sat down and put his elbows on the table.

They needed a sixth person to play the game One Hundred Points. "Want to join us?" Nan asked.

"No poker, boys," Sang said. "Give me something to drink."

Yang Wei poured him a mug of corn liquor. "Here you are," he said, winking at the others.

"Good, this is what I need." Sang raised the mug to his lips and almost emptied it in one gulp. "I came here for serious business tonight."

"What is it?" Daiheng asked.

"I invite you boys over to screw my wife," Sang said deliberately.

All the young men were taken aback, and the room suddenly turned quiet except for the sputtering of the coal stove. They looked at one another, not knowing how to respond.

"You're kidding, Uncle Sang," Daiheng said, after a short while.

"I mean it. She's hot all the time. I want you to give it to her enough tonight." Anger inflamed Sang's eyes.

Silence again fell in the room.

"Afraid to come, huh?" Sang asked, his sparse brows puckered up. A smile crumpled his sallow face.

"Sure, we'd like to come. Who wouldn't?" said Ming, who was a squad leader in the militia.

"Well, sometimes heaven does drop meat pies," Bing said, as if to himself.

"No, we shouldn't go," Nan cut in, scanning the others' faces with his narrow eyes gleaming. He turned to Sang and said, "It's all right to do it to your wife, Uncle Sang, but that could be dangerous to us." Turning to the others, he asked, "Remember what happened at the brickyard last summer? You fellas don't want to get into that kind of trouble, do you?"

His words dampened the heat in the air. For a moment even the squad leader Wang Ming and Liu Daiheng, the oldest of them, didn't know what to say. Everybody remained silent. What Nan had referred to was a case in which a prostitute had been screwed to death by a bunch of brick makers. Of course, prostitution was banned in the New China, but there were always women selling their flesh on the sly. The woman had gone to the brickyard once a month and asked for five yuan a customer, which was a big price, equal to two days' pay earned by a brick maker. That was why the men wouldn't let her off easily. They gave her the money but forced her to work without a stop. As they had planned, they kept her busy throughout the night, and even after she lost consciousness they went on mounting her. She died the next day. Then the police came and arrested the men. Later three of them were sentenced to eight years in prison.

"Nan's right. I don't think we should go," Wei said at last.

"You're no man," Sang said with a sneer, stroking his beardless chin. "I invite you boys to share my wife, free of charge, but none of you dare come. Chickens!"

"Uncle Sang, if you want us to come," Daiheng said, "you ought to write a pledge."

"But I don't know how to write."

"Good idea. We can help you with that," Ming said.

"All right, you write and I'll put in my thumbprint."

Ming went to the desk, pulled a drawer, and took out a pen and a piece of paper. He sat down to work on the pledge.

Nan felt uneasy about the whole thing. How could a husband invite other men to have sex with his wife? he asked himself. I wouldn't. Never. Shuling must've had an affair with someone lately and have been caught by Cuckold Sang. They must've had a big fight today.

Sang was dragging at his pipe silently. Sitting beside him, Bing was putting the poker cards back into the box.

"Here," Ming said, walking over with the paper, "listen carefully, Uncle Sang." Then he read aloud with his eyebrows flapping up like a pair of beetle wings:

> On the third eve of the Spring Festival, I, Sang Zhu, came to the Militia's Office and invited five young militiamen—Hao Nan, Liu Daiheng, Yang Wei, Mu Bing, and Wang Ming—to have sex with my wife Niu Shuling. By doing this, I mean to teach her a lesson so she will stop seducing other men and be a chaste woman in the future. If any physical damage is done to her in the process of the activity, none of the young men shall be responsible. I, Sang Zhu, the husband, will bear all consequences.
>
> The Pledger:
>
> Sang Zhu

Wei placed the ink-paste box on the desk. "Put in your thumbprint if you agree, Uncle Sang."

"All right." Sang pressed his ringworm-nailed thumb into the ink, took it out, blew on its pad, and stamped a scarlet smudge under his name. He wiped off the ink on the leg of his cotton-padded trousers, which were black but shiny with grease stains. Turning away from the table, he blew his nose; two lines of mucus landed on the dusty floor.

"Now, let's go," Ming said, and motioned to the others as though they were going off to bag a homeless dog, which they often did on night patrol.

Nan felt unhappy about the pledge because Ming, the son of a bitch, had put Nan's name first and his own name last among the group, as if Nan had led them in this business. At least, it read that way on paper. He was merely a soldier, whereas Ming was a squad leader.

The snow had stopped, and the west wind was blowing and would have chilled them to the bones if they had not drunk a lot of liquor. Each of them was carrying a long flashlight, whose beam now stabbed into the darkness and now hit a treetop, sending sleeping birds on the wing. They were eager to reach the Sangs', get hold of that loose woman, and overturn the rivers and seas in her. In raptures they couldn't help singing. They sang "I Am a Soldier," "Return to My Mother's," "Our Navigation Depends on the Great Helmsman," "Without the Communist Party There Would Be No New China." In the distance, soundless firecrackers bloomed in the sky over Sea-Watch Village. The white hills and fields seemed vaster than they were in daylight. The first quarter of the moon wandered slowly through clouds among a few stars. The night was clear and quiet except for the men's hoarse voices vibrating.

Nan followed the other men, singing, and he couldn't help imagining what it would feel like to embrace a woman and have her body under his own. He thought of girls in the village, and also of Soo Yan. Though they were engaged, he had never touched her, not even her hand. This was an opportunity to learn how to handle a woman.

They entered Sang's yard. A dark shadow lashed about on the moonlit ground and startled Ming and Daiheng, who were at the front of the group. Then a wolfhound burst out barking at them.

"Stop it!" Sang shouted. "You beast that doesn't know who owns you. Stop it!"

The dog ran away toward the haystack, scared by the beams of the flashlights scraping its body. The yard was almost empty except for a line of colorful washing, frozen and sheeny, swaying in the wind like landed kites tied up by children. Ming tapped on a pink shirt, which was apparently Shuling's, and said, "It smells so delicious. Why no red on this, Old Sang? She's too young for menopause, isn't she?"

They broke out laughing.

Sang's little stone house had a thatched roof. Entering it, they put their two rifles behind the door. An oil lamp was burning on the dining table on the brick bed, but nobody was in. Finding no woman, the men began swearing and said they were disappointed. Sang searched everywhere in the house, but there was no trace of his wife. "Shu—ling—" he cried to the outside. Only the hiss of the wind answered.

"Old Sang, what does this mean?" Daiheng asked. "What do you have in mind exactly?"

"I want you to do it to my wife."

"But where is she?" Bing asked.

"I don't know. You boys wait. I'm sure she'll be back soon."

Sang's eyes were filled with rage. Obviously he didn't expect to see an empty house either. He took a large bowl of boiled pork and a platter of stewed turnips from the kitchen and placed them on the table. They climbed on the brick bed and started eating the dishes and drinking the liquor they had brought along.

"It's too cold," Wei said, referring to the food.

"Yes," Ming said. "Let's have something warm, Old Sang. We have work to do."

"You must treat us well," Bing said, "or else we won't leave tonight. This is our home now."

"All right, all right, you boys don't go crazy. I'm going to cook you a soup, a good one."

Sang and Daiheng went to the kitchen, lighting the stove and cutting pickled cabbages and fat pork. In the village Daiheng was well known as a good cook, so he did the work naturally.

"Don't be stingy. Put in some dried shrimps," Wei shouted at the men in the kitchen.

"All right, we will," Sang yelled back.

Nan remained silent meanwhile. He didn't like the tasteless meat and just kept smoking Sang's Glory cigarettes and cracking roasted melon seeds. In the kitchen the bellows started squeaking.

Ming and Wei were playing a finger-guessing game, which Nan and Bing didn't know how to play but were eager to learn. Nan moved closer, watching their hands changing shapes deftly under the oil lamp and listening to them chanting:

> A small chair has square legs,
> A little myna has a pointed bill.
> It's time you eat spider eggs,
> Drink pee and gulp swill.
>
> Five heads,
> Six fortunes,
> Three stars,
> Eight gods,
> Nine cups—

"Got you!" Ming yelled at Wei. Pointing at a mug filled with liquor, he ordered, "Drink this."

They hadn't finished the second round when Daiheng and Sang rushed in. "She's here, she's here," Daiheng whispered, his voice in a flutter.

Before they could straighten up, Shuling stepped in, wearing a red scarf and puffing out warm air. She whisked the snowflakes off her shoulder with a pair of mittens and greeted the men. "Welcome," she said. She looked so fresh with her pink cheeks and permed hair. Her plump body swayed a little against the white door curtain, as if she didn't know whether she should stay in or go out.

"Well, well, well," Ming hummed.

"Where have you been?" Sang asked sharply, then went up to her and grabbed the front of her sky-blue jacket.

"I, I—let me go." She was struggling to free herself.

"I know where you were. With that pale-faced man again. Tell me, is that true or not?" Sang pulled her closer to himself. He referred to a young cadre on the work team which was investigating the graft and bribery among the leaders of the production brigade. Nan remembered seeing the man and Shuling together in the grocery store once.

"Let me go. You're hurting me," she begged, and turned to the others, her round eyes flashing with fear.

"You stinking skunk, always have an itch in your cunt!" Sang bellowed. "I want you to have it enough today, as a present for the Spring Festival. See, I have five men for you here. Every one of them is strong as a bull." His head tilted to the militia.

"No, don't. Please don't," she moaned with her hands held together before her chest.

"What are you waiting for, boys?" Sang shouted at the young men.

They all jumped up and went to hold her. "Brothers, don't do this to me," she wailed.

"Do it to her! Teach her a good lesson," her husband yelled.

They grabbed her and carried her onto the brick bed. She struggled and even tried to kick and hit them, but like a tied sheep she couldn't move her legs and arms. Daiheng pinched her thigh as Ming was rubbing her breasts. "Not bad," Ming said, "not flabby at all."

"Oh, you hooligans. Let your grandma go. Ouch!"

With laughter, they placed her on the hard bed. She never stopped cursing. "All your ancestors will go to hell. Sons of asses . . . I'll tell your parents. Your houses will be struck by thunderbolts! You'll die without a son . . ."

Her curses only incensed the men. Bing rolled one end of her woolen scarf into a ball and thrust it into her mouth. Instantly she stopped making noises. Then Sang produced some ropes and tied her hands to the legs of the dining table. Meanwhile Wei and Nan did as they were told by Ming, binding her feet to the beam that formed the edge of the bed.

They slipped their hands underneath her underclothes, kneading her breasts and rubbing her crotch. Then they ripped open her jacket, shirts, pants, and panties. Her partly naked body was squirming helplessly in the coppery light.

Daiheng took out five poker cards, from the ace to the "5," mixed them, and then put them on the bed. By turns they picked the cards. Wei had "5," Nan "4," Bing "3," Daiheng "2." As Ming got the ace, he was to go first.

"All right," Sang said calmly, "everything is fine. Now you boys enjoy yourselves." He raised the door curtain and went out.

Ming began to mount Shuling, saying, "I've good luck this

year. Nan, little bridegroom, watch your elder brother carefully and learn how to do it."

Nan was wondering whether Daiheng had contrived a trick in dealing out those cards. How come both Ming and Daiheng had gotten ahead of the three younger men? But he didn't attend to his doubt for long, because soon Ming's lean body was wriggling violently on Shuling's. Having never seen such a scene, Nan felt giddy and short of breath, but he was also eager to experience it. They all watched intently. Meanwhile the woman kept her face away from them.

While Daiheng was on Shuling, biting her shoulders and making happy noises, Sang came in with a small enamel bowl in his hand. He climbed on the bed and placed it beside his wife's head. He clutched her hair and pulled her face over, and said, "Look at what's in the bowl." He picked up a bit of the red stuff with three fingers and let it trickle back into the bowl. "Chili powder. I'll give it to you. Wait, after they are done with you, I'll stuff you with it, to cure the itch in there for good."

His wife closed her eyes and shook her head slightly.

Bing, who was the third, obviously had no experience with a woman before. No sooner had he gotten on top of her than he came and gave up. He held his pants, looking pained, as though he had just swallowed a bowl of bitter medicine. He coughed and blew his nose.

Now it was Nan's turn. He seemed bashful as he moved to Shuling. Though this was his first time, he felt confident as he straddled her and started unbuckling his pants. He looked down at her body, which reminded him of a huge frog, tied up, waiting to be skinned for its legs. Looking up, he noticed that her ear was small and delicate. He grabbed her hair and pulled her face over to see closely what she looked like. She opened her eyes, which were full of sparkling tears and staring at him. He was surprised by the fierce eyes but could not help observing them. Somehow her eyes were changing—the hatred and the fear were fading, and beneath their blurred surfaces loomed a kind of beauty and sadness that was bottomless. Nan started to fantasize, thinking of Soo Yan and other pretty girls in the village. Unconsciously he bent down and intended to kiss that pale face, which turned aside and spilled the tears. His head began swelling.

"What are you doing?" Daiheng shouted at Nan.

Suddenly a burst of barking broke out beyond the window. The wolfhound must have been chasing a fox or a leopard cat that had come to steal chickens. Wild growls and yelps filled the yard all at once.

"Oh!" Nan cried out. Something snapped in his body; a numbing pain passed along his spine and forced him off her. By instinct, he managed to get to his feet and rushed to the door, holding his pants with both hands. Cold sweat was dripping from his face.

Once in the outer room he dropped to his knees and began vomiting. In addition to the smell of the half-cooked cabbage soup in the caldron, the room was instantly filled with the odor of alcohol, sour food, fermented candies, roasted melon seeds. His new cotton-padded shoes and new dacron jacket and trousers were wet and soiled.

"Little Nan, come on!" Daiheng said. Putting his hand on Nan's head, he shook him twice.

"I'm scared. No more," Nan moaned, buckling his belt.

"Scared by a dog? Useless," Sang said, and restrained himself from giving Nan a kick.

"Come on, Nan. You must do it," Ming said. "You just lost your Yang. Go get on her and have it back, or you've lost it for good. Don't you know that?"

"No, no, I don't want to." Nan shook his head, groaning. "Leave me alone. I'm sick." He rubbed his eyes to get rid of the mist caused by the dizziness. His hands were slimy.

"Let that wimp do what he wants. Come back in," Sang said aloud, straddling the threshold.

They went in to enjoy themselves. "Ridiculous, scared by a dog," Wei said, giggling and scratching his scalp.

Holding the corner of the cauldron range in the dark, Nan managed to stand up, and he staggered out into the windy night.

As Ming said, Nan lost his potency altogether. In fact, he lay in bed for two days after that night when he walked home bare-headed through the flying snow. At first, he dared not tell his parents what had happened, but within a week the entire village knew Nan had been frightened by Sang's dog and had lost his Yang. His father scolded him a few times, while his mother wept in secret.

Two weeks later the Soos returned to the Haos the Shanghai wristwatch and the Flying Pigeon bicycle, two major items of the dowry already in Yan's hands, saying Nan was no longer a normal man, so they wouldn't marry their daughter to him. Despite Mrs. Hao's imploring, the Soos refused to keep the expensive gifts. However, they did say that if Nan recovered within half a year they might reconsider the engagement.

For four months Nan had seen several doctors of Chinese medicine in town. They prescribed a number of things to restore his manhood: ginseng roots, sea horses, angelica, gum dragon, deer antler, tiger bones, royal jelly, even a buck's penis, but nothing worked. His mother killed two old hens and stewed them with ginseng roots. Nan ate the powerful but almost inedible dish; the next day he had a bleeding nose and soon began losing his hair. His father cursed him, saying the Hao clan had never had such a nuisance. Indeed, after eating two or three slices of buck's penis, a normal man wouldn't be able to go out because of the erection, but nothing could help Nan. There was no remedy for such a jellyfish.

By now the villagers no longer counted Nan as a man. Children called out, "Dog-Scared," when they ran into him. Though quite a few matchmakers visited the Haos, they all came for his sisters. Among all the unfilial things, the worst is childlessness. But what could Nan do? He had once thought of poisoning Sang's wolfhound, but even that idea didn't interest him anymore. One afternoon when he was on his way to the pig farm, the dog came to him, lashing its tail and wagging its tongue. He wanted to give it a kick, but he noticed Soo Yan walking two hundred meters away along the edge of the spinach field; so instead he threw his half-eaten corn cake to the dog, who picked it up and ran away. Nan watched the profile of that girl. She wore cream-colored clothes, her fiery gauze scarf waving in the breeze. With a short hoe on her shoulder, she looked like a red-crowned crane moving against the green field.

■ Sovereignty

Liao Ming of Horse Village was drinking sorghum liquor in his yard. The dog barked and the front gate opened. Raising his thick eyelids, Liao recognized the visitor and stopped the dog. "What wind brought you here, Old Leng?" he said loudly.

Leng was panting hard, so Liao asked again, "How are things?"

"Not very good, Old Liao," Leng said, coming closer. Sweat was trickling down his forehead and cheeks, and he wiped it off with his soiled hand. That turned his face into an opera-mask, full of streaks. "Old Liao, I came to beg you for help."

"How can I help you?" Liao asked, and tilted his gray head. "Why don't you sit down and have a cup first?"

"No, thanks," Leng said, standing in front of Liao with both hands on his narrow hips. "Vet Bai said today is the best time for my sow, but Ma Ding, the son of a bitch in Willow Village, didn't show up with his boar. He promised me to come at three o'clock. Damn his grandma, I washed my sow and cleaned up everything, waiting for him all the while. It's past four already. My sow can't wait anymore. So . . ."

"So what?" said Liao. He struck a match and lit a new load of tobacco.

"So I came to invite you to help."

"No, no." Liao waved to put out the match and exhaled two lines of smoke. "My boar will have a good time with Mu Bushao's sow tomorrow morning. If he gives all his stuff to your sow today, he'll be empty tomorrow and have nothing left for Mu's sow. No, that won't do. You know, I can't cheat folks of our village. Even a rabbit knows not to eat the grass near its own hole."

"I beg you, Old Liao! Please come, just for the reason we've been neighbors for generations, just for the respect for our old folks who were friends."

"Just for all those, humph? Why didn't you come here in the first place?" Liao's cheeks turned red.

"Forgive me just this once, all right? Next time I'll come to you first." Leng paused, then added, "But to be fair, I'll pay you better. How about fifteen yuan a mating? You know, five yuan more. You can buy two bottles of sorghum liquor for that money."

"Save the five yuan for your mother!" Liao said, and knocked the bronze pot of his pipe against the stone stool under his hips. "You black-hearted men only know money. For a few yuan you'd sell your fathers' coffin lumber. You heard that white foreign pigs grew bigger than our black native pigs, so you all take your sows to Ma Ding for a foreign fucking. Everybody knows white pigs' pork tastes no good, but you don't care. You only want your pigs to grow bigger and weigh more on the scale at the buying station. Where's your heart, man? You can't cheat the buyer, our country, like this!" Whitish foam circled Liao's lips.

"All right, I'm in the wrong, Old Liao. Come on, we have no

time to talk like this. The sow is waiting for you at my home. Please come and finish the business."

"Waiting for me? What makes you think I'll come?"

"I know you will, 'cause you understand things and you're always good to your neighbors. If you don't help me, who will?"

Liao's anger seemed to be fading. He raised the cup and emptied the last drops, but he thrust the pipe into the tobacco pouch and was about to load it again.

"Come on, Brother Liao, I beg you."

"You go first. I'll follow you," Liao said casually. He tied the pouch around the pipe and tucked the package behind his cloth waistband.

"Now I have your word, Old Liao. I'm running back and waiting for you, all right?"

"You can run your doggy legs off. I'll be with you in a couple of minutes."

As soon as Leng disappeared beyond the gate Liao went to a vat beneath the eaves. He scooped out two gourd-ladles of boiled soybeans for his boar. Before every mating he would give it some nutritious food. After all, it labored for him. In recent years it had brought him a profit equal to the amount that two farm-hands could make. The mating business had been very good until Ma Ding got his white foreign boar and became a competitor, but so far Liao still had enough customers. Most households in Horse Village remained loyal to him.

"Big boy, today you're lucky again," he spoke to the boar, which was eating away noisily. "You've luck both for your mouth and your cock. I arrange weddings for you every week, aren't you grateful? You ought to be. You happy pig, your children are spread everywhere. You should work harder for me, shouldn't you?" He rapped the neck of the boar twice, and it snorted back appreciatively.

He brought out a hemp rope and tied it around the boar's neck. The door of the pigpen was lifted and the boar came out. Watching its large body that weighed over three hundred kilos, Liao couldn't help speaking again. "I'm proud of you, boy. You brought me not only cash but also respect among the folks. With one spear you've conquered so many villages. No man can do as much as you did. Now, shall we go?"

"Who are you talking to over there, my old man?" his wife called out from the house.

"To our boar, my old woman. We're leaving to do business. Scramble a dozen eggs for supper. We'll make some extra money today. I'll be back in an hour or so."

"All right, you come back soon. We'll wait for you." The bellows in the kitchen resumed croaking while fat was sputtering in the cauldron.

Liao set out for Leng's house. Rapidly the boar was treading the road, whose surface of dried mud had been cut into numerous ruts by oxcarts. The air was still warm, though the crimson sun was approaching the indigo peak of the Great Emperor Mountain. Grass had pierced the soil here and there, and the cornfields, sown a few days before, looked like huge gray ribs stretching towards the end of the green sky. Everything seemed sluggish and even the air made one feel languid. In the west, a herd of sheep were slowly coming down the mountain slope like clouds lying atop the bushes. Small voices, children's voices, were buzzing from distant places. Once every few seconds a donkey's bray split the air.

Leng's house was at the northern end of Horse Village, within ten minutes' walk. When he arrived, Liao led his boar directly into Leng's yard and closed the gate behind him. He wanted to get the business done quickly, take the pay, and return home for the supper of scrambled eggs, fried dough cakes, soy paste, raw scallions, stewed hairtail, which he bought in Dismount Fort that morning after he had sold a litter of piglets there. He liked that fish best and never could have enough of it.

To his surprise, in the middle of Leng's yard was standing a huge white boar. Beyond it a young sow was lying on her back against a nether millstone. The boar's owner, Ma Ding, whom Liao recognized at a glance, was talking with Leng. Second Dog, Leng's teenage son, was shoveling manure out of the pigpen. Seeing Liao and the black boar, the boy stopped to make a face, a snouty pout, at his father and Ma Ding.

Anger welled up in Liao. I'm taken in, he thought. Leng, you dung-eater, you have Ma here already, ahead of me.

He wanted to walk straight to Leng and give him a round of curses that would make his ancestors squirm in their graves, but he hesitated because right in front of him was the white boar that was so large, even larger than his black boar. Shedding fierce glints, the white boar's lozenge eyes were blinking at Liao and the black boar behind him.

Leng realized the embarrassment he had caused. He stopped talking and turned around, coming over to calm Liao. He had hardly walked a step when Liao yelled out and was thrown to the ground. A black shadow flitted over his body and dashed to the white boar. Both Leng and Ma jumped aside instinctively. Chickens and ducks burst away in every direction, and a rooster landed on the wall, then flew off to the neighbor's yard. Second Dog thrust the shovel into the manure heap and vaulted out of the pigpen, shouting excitedly, "Good pig, get that foreign bastard. Drive him back home!"

The boars' growls, louder than those sent out by a pig in a slaughterhouse when a long knife stabbed into its throat, were vibrating through the neighborhood and the village.

Liao got up to his feet. The two pigs were already in a melee. Though the white boar was bigger and heavier, the black one was nimbler and fiercer. Watching them rolling about, Liao felt his boar was by no means inferior to that white foreign beast. Just now when the fight broke out, by instinct he had wanted to stop them, uncertain if his pig could match its enemy, but now he changed his mind. His boar had to be the master in this village at least. Let him fight to protect his territory, Liao thought, to keep his wives and concubines, to get rid of that foreign bastard, and teach both Ma and Leng a hard lesson. See if they dare to look down on me and my boar again.

Instead of trying to separate the pigs, Liao stood there motionless and enjoyed watching them fighting. Likewise, Ma and Leng seemed also eager to see the fight through. Unlike the men, Second Dog openly took sides, waving a wooden stick to urge the black boar on. They all forgot the sow that had escaped into the pigpen.

The white boar opened its jaws, snapping at its attacker. Its scarlet tongue was dripping blood, which the men couldn't tell was from the wounds on the black boar or from the bleeding inside its own mouth. Again and again its flinty teeth cut through the air but missed the black boar, which seemed clever, able to parry the attacks with its snout.

After a few rounds the two pigs disengaged themselves. Each stepped back for ten feet or so, turned around facing the other for a moment, as if dazed by the hot blood pumped into their heads, then dashed toward each other and clashed with a muffled noise. Neither of them lost its balance or retreated a step. Instead they stuck together, holding each other with their snouts, and started a kind of wrestling. The two bodies turned tense as if having shed their fat. The pigs were circling around and around rather slowly; each wanted to throw the other down, but neither was able to make it. Their columnar hind feet sank into the earth.

Suddenly the black boar passed water. A thick line of greenish liquid gushed out and fell on the ground. Liao's heart shuddered, because he realized his boar couldn't match the white beast in strength. He was right; in a few seconds the black boar began retreating, two deep grooves emerging under its hind feet. The ground soaked with the urine could no longer give a solid footing. The white boar pushed and pushed and pushed, till with a crushing thrust it hurled its enemy over. The black boar collapsed right in front of its master's feet, whining and gasping. Liao felt a sharp pain in his heart and wanted to bend down to help it up, but he restrained himself, seeing a smile cross the square face of Ma Ding, who was looking at the black boar contemptuously. Anger flamed up in Liao and he kicked his pig ferociously in the flank. That sent it to its feet at once. The boar seemed to understand its master's mind and went for its enemy again.

This time they fought differently. The black boar appeared to know its own physical inferiority and tried resorting to its teeth. With its mouth open, it snapped at the white boar, which couldn't move fast enough to avoid every attack. Yet the white boar was so large it stood there like a bridge pier.

Liao worried. Obviously his boar had no chance of winning the fight. While he was figuring how to invent an excuse for withdrawing his force from the battle, the black boar stepped aside; then, approaching the white boar slowly, all of a sudden it jumped into the air with its front legs upwards. The pair of pointed feet plunged and stabbed into its enemy's face. The white boar growled wildly. Below its right eye an inch of hairy skin was torn off together with a chunk of flesh, and the cut, smeared with yellowish mud, turned scarlet instantly.

"Good pig! He sure knows how to scratch," Leng cried.

"Kill this foreign beast," Second Dog shouted, whacking the white boar's rump with the stick.

"Second Dog!" Ma yelled. "You son of a rabbit, don't abuse a pig! It's just a dumb animal."

Liao was pleased. Looking at Ma, he put on a smile and said, "We stop here, Old Ma, all right?"

Ma didn't respond, as though he hadn't heard Liao.

The two pigs went on biting each other. The white boar looked pink now, but there weren't many wounds on its body, and it had gotten only a few short rosy furrows on its sides. Though the black boar didn't change color, it had more wounds than its enemy. Yet its fighting spirit was not sinking. The dark snout reached for the under part of the white belly and took a solid snap at the soft area beneath the ribs. The white boar gave out a deafening howl, and blood was dripping on the ground. The black boar was stunned by the murderous sound and paused, standing there as if wondering. The white boar jumped up into the air and its cavernous mouth dived onto its enemy. The huge pink jaws crushed the dark head and struck the black boar away at least ten feet. Immediately the black boar dashed off growling, and the white boar was chasing behind. None of the men had seen how it had happened—in the dust a black ear, bigger than an open hand, was twitching and twitching like a giant bat.

The black boar rushed into the latrine and came out from the other side. The white boar followed. The poles supporting the latrine were smashed and tossed to the ground. The instant the white boar emerged from the other side the latrine collapsed.

"My outhouse! Oh, my outhouse," Leng cried. "You two stop your pigs. They're destroying my property."

Second Dog picked up a pitchfork and went for the white boar, shouting, "Goddamn it, I'm going to run you through, white beast!"

"No, hold!" Ma yelled and threw up his hands.

"Second Dog, put it down!" his father ordered harshly. The boy froze and dropped the pitchfork.

The pigs couldn't be stopped now. The black boar seemed to be recovering from the giddiness caused by the loss of the ear and stood against the adobe wall. With its entire face covered with blood, it looked so monstrous that the white boar faltered in front of the gruesome pig-face. The black boar sent out a thundering roar to the sky and started charging at the white boar that was shaken a little.

The white boar began to dodge its desperate enemy. Gradually the black boar turned to chasing the white boar, jumping about and biting away at the pink rump and flanks. By now both Liao and Ma wanted to stop the fight, but it was too late, impossible. Nobody dared come close to the pigs, because the black boar was biting at anything within reach. It pursued the white boar so incessantly that the larger pig simply didn't have a chance to stop to put itself together for a real fight.

Then the white boar turned and was headed toward the front gate, the black boar following behind. With a crash the wooden gate disappeared in a cloud of dust.

When the men could see clearly again, both pigs were out of sight. The men ran out and saw them rolling in the wheat field across the road. The white boar now stopped escaping and was engaged in the battle. Wheat seedlings and dark clods were flying around the two pigs that were kicking, jabbing, biting, tearing, grumbling.

As the men were going up to them, both boars stepped back a little, then dashed into each other. The two heads collided with such a clash that both animals staggered and fell to their sides, whining in pain. Around them, the wheat field was scarred with dark patches of soil stripped of the green seedlings.

"We must stop them. They're ruining Sun Fu's crops," Liao said loudly to Ma, Leng, and the villagers who had just arrived to watch.

Leng went back to pick up a plank of the gate. "Give me a hand," he said to Ma. "We'll use this to separate them."

Ma carried the other end of the plank. They walked to the boars, which were knocking at each other with their snouts.

Liao went to pick up the other plank of the gate. With the help of another man, he carried it into the field. They tried the strategy of inserting the plank horizontally between the pigs, and once the two were separated, each plank would hold a boar back. Liao kept approaching them from the side of his own pig, because he thought it knew its master and was less likely to turn upon him. After trying a few times, Liao and his helper succeeded in putting their plank between the pigs. He kept yelling at his boar, "Stop it! Stop, you beast that doesn't know your own parents!"

For a short while the black boar seemed to calm down a little, but it started again. The dark body glided over the plank and landed right on the white boar. With loud growls the two pigs began rolling about again. "Heavens, that black boar wants nothing but death," someone in the crowd said. Second Dog was telling his pals how the white boar had toppled the latrine.

"Hey, you folks," Liao shouted to the crowd, "give us a hand. The pigs have ruined enough things. Do you want the entire field to be turned up?"

Six young men ran over to help. Meanwhile Leng and Ma had managed to insert their plank between the pigs. The other board was immediately put in front of the black boar. Then both planks moved away slowly to separate the pigs as far as possible.

At last the fight was stopped. The two fighters, still whining, were actually too exhausted to continue. Besides, numerous hands were holding them down.

While Ma was tying a rope around his pig's neck, a few youngsters threw stones at the white boar from a distance and shouted in unison, "Foreign pig, go home! Foreign pig, go home!"

"Little turtles," Ma cursed, "my boar must've fucked your teachers pretty bad, or you wouldn't be taught to be so patriotic."

Liao didn't have his rope with him. It must have been in the yard, so he turned to Second Dog, who happened to be close by, and said, "Can you hold this for me for a moment? I'm going to get my rope." The boy took over, holding the corner of the plank and standing by the black boar. He looked at its gory face and felt bad about the ear stump, on which some bluebottles were busy sucking the blood.

Now that Ma had led his pig away, the men holding the black boar let it go. While people were wiping blood and dirt off their hands with wheat seedlings, the black boar sneaked aside and bit Second Dog in the left thigh. The boy was tossed down. A large piece of pale flesh flapped through a triangular gap on his denim pants. He was twisting and gasping on the ground but couldn't cry out. The white bone and the bluish tendons were displayed for quite a while before the astounded villagers could lay their hands on the boy to stop him from writhing in the soil. Meanwhile the black boar was bolting out of the field toward the willow bushes on the bank of the Green Snake Stream.

"Oh, my son!" Leng cried, holding Second Dog in his arms. "Save my boy!"

A leather waistband was immediately tied at the end of the boy's thin thigh, and then a dirty yellow shirt was bound around the wound. In no time the shirt turned crimson. Two men ran off to fetch a tractor; the boy had to be sent to the hospital in Gold County without delay.

Liao returned with his rope. He had been in Leng's yard for a while, looking not only for the hemp rope but also for the pig's ear, which he had not found. Somebody must have stolen it. It couldn't be a dog. Liao suspected Leng's wife had committed the theft. Walking back to the crowd, he swore loudly from a distance, "Whoever stole my pig's ear and eats it will have his bowels busted to ninety-nine pieces!"

"Fuck your grandma!" Leng jumped at Liao, grabbed the front of his jacket and punched him in the face. "Look at what your beast has done to my boy. If only I had a gun, a gun! Oh my, my boy." He burst out crying again. Liao was too stunned to respond. He saw fifty feet away a body twitching slightly in the crowd.

He ran over and looked at the breathless boy on the ground. "Oh my heaven!" His calves cramped, and he couldn't move and had to sit down.

The owner of the wheat seedlings, Sun Fu, arrived. Seeing the field leveled up, his first desire was to pour all kinds of curses on those who were responsible for the damage, but the sight of the injured boy restrained him from doing that. Instead, he went to join the crowd that was talking about the possibility of Second Dog's death.

Liao dared not leave, though his stomach was gurgling. If the boy hadn't been injured, he'd have left without delay for the warm supper at home. But had he done that now, all the villagers would have condemned him and his mating business would have been gone in a matter of days, so he stayed, sincerely hoping to do something, if possible, to comfort the Lengs. Since he couldn't do anything, he kept a low profile, quietly listening to others describing the fight to those who had missed it. Who could imagine pigs were so destructive? Someone suggested the black boar must have had wild blood. By comparison, the white boar seemed tame and less harmful to humans. Maybe white pigs were safer to raise, especially if you had kids.

A tractor arrived ten minutes later and a large cotton blanket was thrown down. The boy was wrapped up and loaded in the trailer. The horn tooted urgently as the tractor was pulling away.

Holding the unconscious boy in her arms in the trailer, Leng's wife cried loudly as though at a funeral. All the way to the hospital, Leng never stopped cursing Liao and Ma and their ancestors. Time and again he thought of ratsbane and swore to himself that he would poison the black boar.

■ Winds and Clouds over a Funeral

Sheng arrived at Gold County to work as a junior clerk in the military department at a large textile mill. Five days later he was informed that his grandmother had passed away. The departmental chief gave him three days to attend the funeral at home. Sheng went to the bus station at noon and got on a bus bound for Dismount Fort.

He used to enjoy seeing the landscape outside the county town, especially the long reservoir that supplied water for six counties, and the large concrete dam that blocked the gorge of a valley and connected two rocky hills. In the middle of the dam stood a small house like a pillbox with loopholes. When the bus crept down the winding road along the bank, the water would flash like large fish scales in the sun. But today Sheng had no appetite for scenery. He closed his eyes and tried to take a cat-nap. He didn't feel very sad, though he loved his grandmother.

Four months before, when he returned home from the army, his grandmother had been so sick that few people thought she would survive the spring. At that time Sheng was waiting at home to be assigned a job, so he was free and could look after her. Every day he talked with her and fed her; occasionally he washed her clothes. He also worked part-time. In the morning, together with a group of youngsters and old men, he loaded bricks onto trucks at a kiln. It was hard work, and in three months he made six hundred yuan—a large sum. He gave all the money to his mother, who saved it for him, or rather, for his wedding, though he didn't have a fiancée yet. Since his father, Ding Liang, was the chairman of the commune, it wasn't diffi-cult for Sheng to find a full-time job in his hometown, but he preferred to go to Gold County.

Gradually, his grandmother recovered, could move about, and even began to cook for the household again. People were amazed and would say to her, "You're lucky to have a good grandson looking after you." She would smile and nod to agree.

In late February when she was very ill, she had thought she was dying. One evening she asked the entire family—her son, daughter-in-law, and grandson—to come to her bedside. She spoke to them calmly, "I'm dying. I have nothing to regret in my life. I've eaten whatever I wanted to eat and enjoyed a lot of ease and comfort. Death is death. When I'm dead, everything will be over for me. Don't miss me. Don't think of me. Just go on with your life." She paused, then resumed, "But I have a wish. I want to be buried after I'm dead. I don't want to be burned. Don't take me to the crematory. I don't want to go there. You don't have to buy me a coffin. Just put me in a wooden box, nail it tightly, and bury it deep in the earth. Remember, deep in the earth, so that no tractor can plow me out when it turns the soil."

"Don't talk like this, Mom," Ding Liang said. "You'll be well soon."

Yuanmin, the daughter-in-law, began sobbing.

"I want you to promise not to burn me," the old woman insisted.

"All right, I promise," Ding said without second thoughts.

Usually in the beginning of a year, quite a few old people died; if one could survive the spring there would be no problem for the rest of the year. Sheng was a little surprised by his grandmother's death in the early summer. But he didn't take it hard, for he was a young man hardened by his four years' service in the army, where he had seen his comrades killed in live-ammunition maneuvers. His grandmother had lived eighty years; her death was like a ripe nut that falls.

Yet his mind couldn't help turning to the burial, because nowadays the government encouraged people to cremate the dead in order to preserve arable land. Recently an editorial in the Party's newspaper, *The People's Daily,* said that in a hundred years there would be no land for growing crops if ground burials were not stopped. "We have to be responsible," the article said, "not only for the dead but, more important, for the children to come. It is our duty to leave them an unclogged land."

When Sheng reached home, there were a dozen people from the neighborhood in the yard. They were busy helping the Dings prepare the funeral, which was scheduled for next morning, since the hot weather made it impossible for the body to stay home for long. Under an awning in front of the house lay an old black coffin on small stools; Sheng was told that his grandmother's body was inside. Two rows of wreaths with consolatory words on them stretched before the coffin, forming a fan-shaped space. His mother, red-eyed, came and secured a crepe around his right arm with safety pins. She told him, "Your grandma didn't suffer.

This morning we found her still in bed. We called her. She didn't answer. She was dead for a while. Just slept to death." Tears trickled down her cheeks, and she wiped them off.

"It's a happy ascent," said Uncle Wang, who lived next door.

"This old woman was blessed," said a middle-aged woman, a colleague of Yuanmin's. "Without any suffering, such a clean, peaceful death. I hope I'll die in the same way."

Sheng felt a little comforted. His father came and put a hand on his shoulder. "Don't be too sad," he told Sheng. "It's time for her to go. She had a good life."

Sheng nodded, feeling they shouldn't be treating him as though he were a young boy. Then his father pulled him aside and said in a low voice, "I've told the Carpentry House to prepare a coffin. They don't make coffins for the market anymore. We borrowed this one from them." He pointed at the old coffin. "The new one will be ready tomorrow, but they don't have good wood, only pine and aspen. We chose pine for her."

"That's all right. How much does it cost?"

"About a hundred and fifty."

Sheng knew that was cheap, at a big discount, but his parents didn't have the money. Though they both worked, they had a large debt. Fifteen years before, Sheng's aunt, his father's only sister, had gone mad and been sent to a mental hospital in Dalian City. Because she was unmarried at that time and he was the only man in the family, Ding had to pay for the expenses. He borrowed the money from the commune. Not until a few months before had the debt been cleared, but the Dings had not yet recovered from many years' straits. Now, in addition to the coffin, there would be other expenses, such as the new clothes, cigarettes, wine, tea, candies, food, wreaths, and at least one feast.

Sheng found his mother in the kitchen and told her to use the money he had made at the kiln. Some neighbors overheard what he said. "Yuanmin," an old woman praised, "what a good son you have!" Her words made Sheng blush a little.

His mother smiled and said, "His grandma died a timely death, as if she waited for her grandson to come home to look after her and make the money for her funeral."

Sheng gave a thought to that. Somehow he felt his mother was right; it looked as though everything had mysteriously fallen into place. He turned and saw a pile of small steamed buns in a large basket. "What are these for?" he asked.

"For kids," his mother said. "A lot of them come to steal a bun, because your grandma lived eighty years. Their parents think the buns from us can make the kids live longer, so they tell them to come here and steal some."

Sheng remembered eating such a bun when he was ten. He picked up a dozen or so and carried them out to refill the plates at the head of the coffin.

It was getting dark. He sat on a low bench beside the coffin. Four more wreaths had been added to the rows since he came home. He noticed some clothing, perhaps his grandmother's sheets and quilts, hanging on the fence, but they were almost torn to rags. A young woman was busy cutting the clothes with scissors. He stood up and was about to stop her, but Uncle Wang intervened, "Let her take a piece, Sheng. Your grandma was a blessed woman. That's why they want a piece of her clothes to put into their babies' quilts, to make the kids easier to raise."

Then the old man described to Sheng how their roof had been covered with birds that morning. Thousands of swallows, sparrows, doves, and magpies landed on the house. Even the electric wires were fully occupied. People were amazed and thought that the birds were angels who had come down to fetch the dead, and that the old woman must have done a lot of good works in her life.

Together with the men who were either the family's friends or grateful to his father, Sheng was to keep vigil beside the coffin. He took out some candles and joss sticks for repelling mosquitoes. On the narrow table along the coffin were a basket of steamed bread stuffed with pork and garlic bolts, cups filled with green tea, plates containing Peony cigarettes, roasted peanuts, toffee, and haw jelly. The Dings had to be very generous on this occasion.

At seven in the evening Huang Zhi, a vice-chairman of the commune, called at the Dings. After giving his condolences, he followed the host into the inner room with a teacup in his hand. "Old Ding," Huang said uneasily, "I heard that the Carpentry House is preparing a coffin for your mother. Is that true?"

"Well, news travels fast, doesn't it?" Ding Liang said with a bitter smile.

"Old Ding, I don't mean to interfere with your family affairs, but as a colleague I should advise you to think it over before you bury your mother."

"What have you heard exactly?"

"Secretary Yang told me about the coffin. You see, you ought to think of the consequence."

"Damn his grandmother, he'll never leave me alone. Even if he rules heaven and earth, he can't rule things in my household."

"Chairman Ding, I don't mean I agree with Secretary Yang on everything, but I do think you should take into account the political effect of your mother's burial. You are the head of the commune. Thousands of eyes are staring at you."

"You mean I should burn my mother?"

"I don't mean that. In fact, I came to inform you that we're going to have a Party meeting tonight and discuss this matter. Please come at eight."

"A Party meeting to discuss how to get rid of my mother's body?"

"No hard feelings, Old Ding. This is a decision made by the Party committee. I'm here only to deliver the message and make sure you will be present."

"All right, I'll come."

In fact, Huang was not Ding's enemy in the Commune Administration. He always sat on the fence. That was why he had been sent to notify Ding of the meeting, which the men of Ding's own faction wanted to hold more eagerly than others. Secretary Yang was on bad terms with Ding and had his own men. The two factions were almost equal in power and would fight over whatever involved their interests and by any means except for assassination. As a precaution, however, the Dings would dump the edibles given to them by those who belonged to the opposite faction whenever they suspected there was poison in them.

At eight Ding arrived at the Commune Administration on Bank Street. The other six committee members were already in the conference room, waving fans and drinking tea. Ding was not afraid of such a meeting, since two men here, Feng Ping and Tian Biao, were loyal to him. Though Yang was the Party chief in the commune, he had only one man on the committee, Dong Cai, who obeyed him like a dog. The other two members, Huang Zhi and Zhang Meng, were fence-sitters and would trim their sails according to the wind.

After they gave condolences to Ding, the meeting started.

While the secretary was introducing the topic, Ding was some-how bewildered, seeing that Yang seemed uninterested in this matter. He had expected Yang would jump at him and criticize him severely for having the coffin made.

"In short," Yang said, "I think this belongs to family affairs. We should let Old Ding decide by himself. Now everybody may express his opinion."

Ding couldn't understand why all of a sudden the secretary appeared to be so gentle and sympathetic. Then his own man, Tian, began to speak. "I agree that it's a private matter, and Chairman Ding has the right to decide on his own. But as the head of the commune, he ought to think of the consequences, the political effect. What will we do if lots of commune members begin to follow Chairman Ding's example and refuse to cremate the dead?"

"I agree," said Feng, who was also Ding's man. "I think the political consequence is enormous. We can't afford to let our leader make such a mistake."

Ding was unhappy about his men's performance. Why do they all turn against me today? he asked himself. They all have a mother. Could they burn their mothers' bodies? I can bury my mother secretly without a ceremony. Few people will know where. I just don't want to burn her up. I promised her not to do that.

While Ding was lost in his thoughts, Dong Cai, Yang's man, began to speak: "I agree with Secretary Yang. I think this is a personal matter that we shouldn't interfere with. We all have old parents. I wouldn't have my mother cremated if she died. That would wreck my family's fortune; at least my father would think so. No, never."

"Thank you," Ding said, so grateful that he couldn't contain himself anymore. "I promised her not to burn her body! Before she died, she begged me with tears not to do that. She just wanted to be buried somewhere deep in the earth. I won't take any arable land."

The meeting dragged on for an hour without reaching a decision. Finally, the secretary proposed a vote, not on whether to bury or cremate the dead but on whether to let Ding choose himself. The result was 4 to 3, in favor of personal choice. Ding felt relieved.

Without saying good night to his men, Ding set out for home. When he turned at the corner of Old Folk Road, Feng and Tian emerged from the side entrance of the Commune Administration. They called Ding and wanted to have a word with him.

"Chairman Ding," Tian said, "do you trust a bastard like Dong Cai or us?"

"Of course I trust you."

"We've followed you for years," Feng said. "We know you are a good, filial man. But they don't think so. Don't be taken in by them. They want you to make a mistake and then they'll jump at you and rip you apart."

"Well, how come?"

"They set a trap for you, Chairman Ding," Tian said, his narrow eyes glittering. "If you bury your mother tomorrow morning, I'm sure they will report you to the higher-ups tomorrow afternoon. To prevent ground burials is a major political task this year, you know that. In fact, Secretary Yang didn't want to hold tonight's meeting. It was Feng and I who persuaded Huang Zhi and Zhang Meng to propose the meeting. They just want to see you fall into a well and then they'll stone you to death, but we want to stop you before you fall."

"Yes," Feng said, "as the saying goes: 'Loyal words jar on your ears—bitter medicine is good for your illness.' We don't want to please but save you."

Ding was shocked. He held out his hands and laid them on both Feng's and Tian's shoulders and said, "My friends, I just realized the true intention behind their sympathy. At the meeting I was too emotional to see through them. I'm grateful for your timely words, which made me stop before it was too late. All right, I will follow your advice." He paused to think for a moment, then said resolutely, "Please help me arrange with the crematory for the service tomorrow morning. Do it tonight, my friends."

Having watched Feng and Tian disappear in the dark, Ding turned and went his way home. A cicada was chirring sleepily in the clear night, and someone was piping a bamboo flute in the distance. By now Ding knew that he had no choice, and that his official career would have been ruined if he had given his mother a ground burial at this moment when the superiors were eager and ready to punish someone so as to check the trend of ground burials. But he had promised his mother. How could he convince his family that the change was reasonable? There would be little trouble with his wife, since she understood such a matter and wouldn't insist on a ground burial; besides, the dead was his mother, not her own flesh and blood. The trouble would come from his son, who had heard him promise the old woman and might not understand how serious this matter was.

Ding was right. When he broke the new decision to the family, Sheng wouldn't accept it. "You promised her yourself. How can she rest in peace if we burn her up?"

"Yes, it's true I promised her," Ding said, trying to be as calm as possible. "Remember what she said about death? She said,

54 ■ Under the Red Flag

'When I am dead, everything will be over for me.' She can't feel anything now. What matters is us, the remaining ones. We have to live and work." Reasonable as he sounded, Ding felt his voice lacking the force it should have.

"Sheng, your dad is right," Yuanmin said.

"No." Sheng shook his head. "A ground burial is the least thing we can do for her." He turned to his father. "I know it may keep you from being promoted, but at worst you'll be demoted one rank."

"Damn it, it's not a matter of demotion or promotion. Those bastards, they want to bury me together with your grandma. Don't you understand? They want to destroy us!"

"Don't yell at each other, please," Yuanmin begged.

As the son couldn't be persuaded, the father proposed a vote. Certainly the wife agreed with the husband, but Sheng wouldn't give up. He mentioned his aunt in Shandong, who was also a family member and should be a voter. "That's ridiculous," Ding said. "Even though we send her a telegram tomorrow morning, it'll take two days to get her word back. Do you want your grandma's body to rot in the heat?"

Seeing that his son couldn't answer, Ding said in a soft voice, "I'm not a dictator in our family. The minority is subordinate to the majority. That is the principle of democracy, isn't it? Our family must unite together in a crisis like this, at least in appearance. I have sent a letter to your aunt and she may come soon. Once she's here, I will explain everything to her. I'm sure she won't be as stubborn as you are."

Sheng knew it was no use arguing. Besides, he was not certain whether his father was totally unreasonable. He went out and sat down on a bench beside the coffin. Several men were dozing away in the candlelight. The night had grown quiet, except that in the distance a pulverizer was humming away in the Harvest Fertilizer Plant. Sheng remembered his grandmother's words and wondered if everything really ended when a person died. Don't we have a soul? he asked himself. If we don't, why do these wreaths say: "May the Spirit of the Departed Remain Forever?" Why do we visit those tombs of the revolutionary martyrs every spring? Why do the folk present dishes, pour wine, and burn paper money before the graves of their family members? If one has a soul, then how does it feel when the body is destroyed, burned? Does the cremation hurt the soul?

Too sleepy, he couldn't focus his mind on any of these questions, which gradually faded away. Soon he began dozing off in the starlit night, like the other men.

Early next morning a junior clerk in the Propaganda Department came with a camera and took some pictures of the wreaths, the coffin, the awning, the men and women in mourning. At nine, two Liberation trucks and a Great Wall van pulled up in front of the Dings'. A dozen young men got off the vehicles and began to load the coffin onto a truck. All the neighbors and friends who wanted to go to the crematory climbed on the other truck, whereas the Dings and a few women who had helped with the needlework took the van.

The crematory was on the western outskirts of Dismount Fort, on the bank of the Blue Brook. A tall chimney stood atop a knoll and spat out thin, whitish smoke whenever the furnace burned. Seeing the ghostly cloud, the old people in town would say, "They are burning a body again. That soul will come back and haunt their homes and lure their children into the marshes." But day by day there were more bodies burned over there, and everyone could tell the business was booming. Young people knew that was where they would have to end up, but they didn't seem to care, since there were so many things to worry about.

The coffin was unloaded in front of the furnace house, and the body was taken out and placed on a narrow, long carriage. Sheng saw his grandmother for the first time after her death. She wore black clothes; everything was brand-new, even the felt hat, the sheets, the quilts. Her pale face was swollen, but she looked very calm, as though in sleep. People began to gather into a line to show their final respect for the old woman. To the Dings' surprise, Secretary Yang, Dong Cai, and several other men of the enemy faction also turned up at the crematory. A few bluebottles were buzzing and circling above the dead face, and Yuanmin waved a handkerchief to keep them away.

Two workmen came and pushed the carriage away to the furnace. The Dings were told that the best kerosene would be used, and that if they wanted to watch they should go to the left-hand side of the furnace and view the cremation through a small hole. Several friends and the Dings moved to the spot; then the carriage was pushed in. The worker pressed the buttons on the handles, and the body and the clothes fell on the floor in the furnace. The moment the carriage came out, flames sprang up from every direction and swallowed the clothes and the body. The viewers could hardly see anything, only fire dancing and swirling before their eyes. Ding Liang couldn't contain himself any longer and burst into a cry, "Oh, Ma, I'm sorry! I'm a bad son. Ma, you wait. Don't go so fast." Tears flowed down his pudgy face. His wife and son began crying too.

Their wailing seemed contagious. Within half a minute the whole furnace room was ringing with the sound of crying, and the floor was sprinkled with tears. People were weeping and blowing their noses. Even Secretary Yang lost self-control, using a handkerchief to wipe his eyes. Some women were supporting each other with their arms while sobbing. Their faces were disfigured by the pain and sadness that suddenly prevailed among the crowd. Only the workmen, who were jaded by this kind of mourning, appeared emotionless. They were smoking quietly. One of them was wiping the ash box on a table with a towel.

Twenty minutes later the flames grew lower and lower as the whirring in the furnace stopped. By and by, an empty chamber could be seen through the small hole. A worker opened the furnace, in which remained a layer of ashes that looked like broken clamshells. Another workman used a poker to gather everything into a large shovel. Then he poured the ashes into a sieve to get rid of the cinders. People began to move out, while the Dings were putting the ashes into the box of sandalwood.

The clerk raised his camera and shot half a dozen pictures, in which the Dings stood against the tall chimney and the neat rows of pines, holding the ash box that had the old woman's portrait and name on its front. By custom, the ashes should be left at the crematory for a month, so the father and the son, who carried the box, went to the small house where the dead souls were stored temporarily. Once inside, they saw dozens of boxes on the shelves that had been set up along the walls. The floor was littered with bread, fruits, colorful paper, burned joss sticks, dog and human feces. They placed the box on top of a shelf and went out for fresh air. Although the place was untidy, they felt it was bearable, since they would take the old woman home soon.

Then the whole crowd climbed on the trucks, which carried them to East Wind Inn, where Yuanmin worked as the vice-manager. There they would have the feast, for which the inn had butchered two pigs. Everybody was welcome. The food was not fancy, only plain rice and four dishes—fried eggplant, pork stewed in soy sauce, tomatoes with scrambled eggs, and cabbage salad—but there was plenty of meat and liquor. Yuanmin paid two hundred and fifty yuan for all the expenses, because she didn't want to give a handle to the Yang faction.

Three days after Sheng had returned to Gold County, an article appeared in *Evergreen News,* Dismount Fort's town paper. It was entitled "Between the Party's Principle and a Son's Filial Duty." It reported on the funeral affairs in detail, describing the old woman's wish to be buried and Chairman Ding's integrity in upholding the Party's policy by refusing his mother a ground burial. Though full of praise, the article had a lot of overtones. Between the lines, an explicit message was conveyed to the reader: Ding Liang was an unfilial son who had burned up his mother in spite of her imploring. It went so far as to say, "Ever since the ancient times, official integrity and family duty have been on contradictory terms. Chairman Ding resolutely sacrificed his old mother to prove his loyalty to the Party and our country."

After reading the article, Ding threw the paper down and flew into a rage. His face turned red, and his big eyes flashed. If he could grab hold of Secretary Yang, he would strangle him.

His anger wouldn't go away even if he ate Yang's crooked heart. Everyone has a mother, but Yang acted as if he came from a pumpkin. Let him wait, wait for the day when his old mother went west.

That night Ding held a secret meeting in the Commune Guest House on West Street. Both Feng and Tian were present. In addition to them was the head of the Propaganda Department, Shao Bin, who was the best writer and painter in town and had recently switched sides, from Yang's faction to Ding's. After a round of Golden Orchid wine, Ding took the newspaper out of his pocket and put it on the table. He said, "Brothers, you know what's in the paper, don't you?"

Everybody nodded without a word. "Damn their ancestors!" Ding cursed. "They are screwing me. If I buried my mother they would report me to the higher-ups. Now my mother has been burned up, they begin bad-mouthing me. Whatever I do, they want to do me in. This world was not made for both Yang Chen and us, and he won't share the same sky with us!"

"I thought they would relent this time, especially after you feasted them," Tian said. "At the crematory I saw Dong Cai, the son of a snake, wiping his eyes with paper. I was amazed that he could have a sympathetic heart. Now his tears turned out to be a trick." Tian took a bite of the chicken leg in his hand.

"We have to figure out a way to fight back," Feng said, spitting watermelon seeds into his palm. "It seems that this time we'll have a war of pens."

"Young Shao," Ding asked, "what do you think we should do?"

"We should write articles to correct the readers' wrong impression given by this one." Shao pointed at the paper on the table.

"I think we must take the high ground," said Tian, who had been a company political instructor in the army. "We shouldn't engage them in the same paper. We'd better begin with big papers. If we have articles published in big papers, they will be silenced automatically, because they dare not oppose a higher body's mouthpiece."

Ding nodded, impressed by the bright idea. Then the meeting proceeded to focus on what kind of articles should be written and to what papers they should be sent. They all agreed that the emphasis should fall on the old woman's change of mind, which had resulted from Chairman Ding's effort to enlighten her on the Party's concern and on the interests of the future generations. The articles would be sent simultaneously to Beijing, Shenyang—the provincial capital—and Gold County. Since Shao was a regular contributor to several newspapers, he assured Ding that he knew where to send the articles.

"Brothers," Ding said to conclude, "a good man needs three helpers, as a pavilion has at least three pillars. I'm grateful to you. If I have wealth and rank someday, I won't forget you, my good brothers."

That very night, Shao Bin roused two junior clerks in his department, and together they set about writing the articles.

Sooner than anyone expected—a week later—*Liaoning Daily*, the biggest provincial newspaper, published an article about the funeral. Although the contents had been changed a great deal from what Shao had written, it provided the ammunition that the Ding faction needed badly. The changed title was more resonant: "For the Happiness of Ten Thousand Generations." The story reported that an old progressive woman in a commune town, called Dismount Fort, had volunteered to have her body cremated after her death, even though her family had prepared an expensive coffin for her. She wanted to leave a clean world for the children to come; for her, that was her best gift for future generations. The paper also printed the picture of the Dings holding the ash box in front of the crematory.

Ding was stunned by the article. He had thought that at best the county's paper might be interested in the funeral, since he had a few influential friends in the county town and he was not unknown to the local media. Now, obviously, the funeral had attracted the attention of the officials in the provincial capital. Far from the truth though this report was, it gave him what he needed at this moment: an authoritative version for the funeral affairs. Facing that, no one in the Yang faction would dare to challenge his loyalty to the Party and his devotion to his mother again. All Ding needed to do now was repeat what the paper said. He ordered the writers in his faction to stick with this definitive version. From now on, all the guns must have the same caliber.

Though the external crisis was eased, the trouble within the family still persisted. Ever since the old woman died, Yuanmin had not slept well at night. She had her own worries. On the day before her mother-in-law's death she took away the old woman's key to the large red chest that contained candies, cookies, and canned fruits. Because Ding was a prominent man in the town, whoever had called on him brought a gift to his sick mother. Sometimes a box of pastry, sometimes a bag of fruits, sometimes a chunk of cooked meat. The red chest was always full of dainties. The old woman opened it several times a day, even at night before she went to bed. That was why she had said, "I've eaten whatever I wanted to eat."

Since it was not healthy to go to bed with a full stomach, Yuanmin was determined to break the bad habit. People ate to work, what was the use of the rich food in the old woman's stomach while she was sleeping? It would only make her fat. The night before her death, Yuanmin said to her, "Mom, give me the key. You mustn't stuff yourself before you go to bed. It will ruin your health."

"No," the old woman said, "what's in the chest is mine. No, I won't give it to you."

Seeing it impossible to bring her around, Yuanmin fished the key out of the jacket hung on the wall. Her mother-in-law started to cry, but Yuanmin wouldn't give it back. Though the old woman planned to tell her son when he came home, she tired of crying and fell asleep.

Yuanmin dared not tell her husband what she had done. If he had known, he would have yelled at her, "You sent her to death!" How could she bear the blame for the rest of her life?

Though she didn't mean to hurt her mother-in-law, the old woman must have hated her at the last moment. If only she had known that was her last day! She would have done anything to please her and let her eat to her heart's content. It was too late now. She didn't love her mother-in-law a lot, but she didn't hate her enough to hurt her. No matter how remorsefully she cried at the funeral, the harm had been done, the wounded soul would never forgive her. She found herself tossing in bed for hours every night.

More frightening than that was her sister-in-law, Shufen, who would arrive in a few days. That country woman had been demented. If she found out what had happened or was unhappy about the cremation, Shufen would fly into a rage and might have a relapse. Then the Dings would have to send her to the mental hospital again. That would mean another huge debt. Yuanmin was terrified to think of it. She remembered that fifteen years before, Shufen had been here, raving, singing, swearing, and laughing in the yard. Sometimes she would run through the streets, imitating a dog's barking, a donkey's braying, a duck's quacking, a sheep's bleating, a rooster's crowing. Children followed her, throwing stones at her. At meals she would stuff herself with whatever she liked without touching anything else, and nobody dared dissuade her. Once she ate a whole bowl of stewed ham and then blasted curses at Yuanmin because while she had been eating, Yuanmin had said, "Sister, why don't you have some rice?"

At that time, the old woman was still alive; whenever Shufen messed her pants or fell into a public latrine, her mother would wash her and the soiled clothes. But now, if she went mad again, Yuanmin would have to take care of everything. It was horrifying to imagine it. She grew so nervous she cried in front of her husband several times. Ding seemed to understand his wife's mind, and he promised that he would handle his sister once she was here for the short visit, but Yuanmin must not provoke her in any way. He tried to comfort his wife, saying that as Shufen hadn't been demented by the death of her husband five years before, it was unlikely that she would have a relapse this time.

After reading the article in *Liaoning Daily*, Sheng felt outraged. How come the whole thing was reversed now? His grandmother had never wanted to be cremated in the first place, and there had never been "an expensive coffin." Lies, newspapers always tell lies, he said to himself. But he was mature enough to keep the anger and the questions to himself. His experience in the army had taught him that disaster always comes from the tongue.

This morning his father telephoned him and asked him to come home to see his aunt, who had just arrived. Sheng got permission from the leaders. Having saved a weekend, he would be able to stay home for two days. He took the three o'clock train. It was only an hour's trip.

When Sheng reached home, his father was in the yard, reading *The Hero and the Eagle,* a chivalric novel. "Was the train crowded?" Ding asked pleasantly, and put the book into his pocket.

"No, I had a window seat."

"Listen," his father said in a low voice, "your aunt will stay here just for a few days. We'll try to do everything to keep her undisturbed. Don't tell her what really happened, all right?"

"Why?"

"I don't want her to go mad again. Do you?"

"Of course not."

"Then just repeat what I tell her. I know her temper better than you do."

"All right."

When Sheng stepped in the house, Shufen was helping Yuanmin cut celery in the kitchen. To Sheng's surprise, his aunt hadn't changed a bit: the same thick, dark hair coiled on top of her head, the same broad, chafed face, the same bulging eyes shooting eerie flashes. Her laugh was as hearty as her body was stout. She saw Sheng and said loudly, "Big nephew, I didn't think you're so tall, a big man now."

"How are you, aunt?"

"Good, I'm good."

Soon dinner was ready. The family sat down at the table while Sheng was pouring White Mountain wine, first for his aunt, then for his father, his mother, and himself. Before they began to eat, Chairman Ding straightened his back a little and spoke with a broad smile. "I am very happy today. First, my sister came. I haven't seen you for fifteen years, Shufen. This is a happy reunion. Second, I was just told that I have been promoted vice-magistrate of Gold County." He turned to Shufen. "I owe my luck to Mother."

Glasses clinked and laughter filled the room while spoons and dishes jingled continuously. Sheng was overwhelmed by his father's announcement. It was a big promotion, which also meant a lot to him. Now his life and future in the county town would be different. His father wouldn't have to help him overtly. Just by having his old man in the County Administration, Sheng would become somebody in his leaders' eyes. They wouldn't dare ask him to buy soy oil for them through the back door again. Instead, they would think of what to offer him on holidays. And the pretty girls in the textile mill; he would marry the prettiest of them and settle down in the big county town. He had never thought fate would favor him this way. Emboldened by the good wine, he stood up and said, "Dad, congratulations!"

They drank up. Then Ding turned to Shufen and said, "Sis, you have seen those pictures of the funeral and the newspapers. We did want to bury Mother. But she wanted to be with us forever, so we had her cremated without waiting for your word."

"My word is worthless," Shufen said. "You're her son."

"Don't be angry with me, sis. You see, only by putting her into a small box can we take her with us wherever we go. I'm a cadre in the Party and can be sent to any part of the country. If we buried her here, we'd have to leave her in the wilderness alone. We can't do that."

"Brother, don't get me wrong. You don't need to persuade me. I can see you've done everything you can. The wreaths, the pictures, the articles in the papers, what else would our mother want? It was a big funeral; every part of it was big. If she was at our home village, we couldn't do anything like that. Our mother's soul must be happy in heaven now."

What a relief Yuanmin experienced! Not knowing how to express it in words, she picked up a large piece of braised pig ear and put it in her sister-in-law's plate.

"Wait a minute," Shufen said. "I must take something home."

Yuanmin withdrew her chopsticks with a start. Shufen went on, "I want to take all the pictures with me, to show them to our neighbors. Brother, do you remember Uncle Liu?"

"Yes, I remember that old man."

"He died last year and had only two wreaths. Two wreaths." She drew a pair of large circles in the air with her chopsticks. "But our mother had thirty-six. I want to show them."

Ding laughed and assured his sister that she could have all the photographs, together with the glossy album. Yuanmin promised her that they would mail her more. Then Ding announced that next morning Sheng would accompany his aunt to the crematory and bring the old woman back home. Though it was not a month yet, it didn't matter. They wanted to place the ash box in the main room so that they could worship her on holidays and set a bowl for her whenever they had a good meal.

Sheng knew that not every word his father said was true, but he was convinced that the funeral affairs had to be handled this way. Now he realized what a powerful, experienced father he had, a father who could act according to circumstances and could prosper in adversities. He felt there was a lot to learn from his old man. Again he stood up and raised his glass. "Dad, congratulations!"

■ The Richest Man

In our town the richest man was Li Wan. Once an army doctor, he was demobilized in 1963. Since then, he had been a physician in the Commune Clinic, where his wife also worked, as a nurse. He had a nickname, Ten Thousand, which referred to the amount he had in the bank. Years before, his nickname had been different: people called him Thousand, because at that time his savings had not yet reached five figures.

Li was a miser. The whole town talked about how stingy he was. There were many anecdotes of him: he used soda ash for toothpaste and soap; he made a rule for his wife that she must not put in more than four tiny dried shrimps when she cooked noodles; instead of buying a packet, he always bought four or five cigarettes at a time; he stored a lot of corn husks at home as toilet paper. Of course, frugality is a virtue. Everybody understands that, just as the last page of a household's grain booklet reminds us:

> From every meal you save a mouthful,
> In a year you will have many a bushel.

But with his monthly salary of 110 yuan, almost twice a common worker's, Li ought to be openhanded. He shouldn't have haggled with egg and vegetable vendors in the marketplace as if he were buying an ox, and once in a while he ought to do his neighbors a small favor, like giving a kid a pencil on Children's Day or an old man a stalk of sugar cane at the Mid-Fall Festival. No, he had never done anything like that. He had yet to learn how to give. That is indeed a difficult thing for a wealthy man to do.

In addition, few men can be rich without being arrogant. Li Wan was no exception. Though niggardly by nature, he could be extravagant. He had the best fowling piece—the only double-barreled gun in town, a German camera, and a Yellow River motorcycle. There was another man in Dismount Fort who owned a motorcycle, but that man, a welder in the Harvest Fertilizer Plant, was a fool. He rode the thing only for vanity and told all women who didn't know him that he was an engineer. In Li's case, these pieces of property showed substantial wealth. Li allowed nobody to touch his motorcycle and never gave anyone a ride.

Without the distinction between the high and the low, there would be no sorrow; without the difference between the rich and the poor, everyone could be contented. How wise is that ancient saying. The whole town hated Li, whose stinginess and extravagance made people's lives unbearable. They all agreed that he deserved to be childless.

When the Cultural Revolution broke out, however, the two most powerful mass associations in town, the Team of Maoism and the League of Mao Zedong Thought, tried to enroll Li, not because he was rich but because he had once been a revolutionary officer. Besides, he was a doctor, useful to a mass organization, especially when it resorted to cudgels, swords, guns, grenades, and mines against its enemy. Li refused to join either of the associations, and his arrogance outraged the enthusiastic masses. As Chairman Mao instructs: "If you are not a friend of the people, you are an enemy of the people."

Naturally some men in the League of Mao Zedong Thought began to think how to punish Li Wan. That was not easy, because Li was from a poor peasant family, was a Party member, and seemed to be red inside and out. Nonetheless they kept an eye on him and assigned a young man, Tong Fei, to prepare a file and collect material against him. While the whole town was busy making revolution, how could they tolerate a man who would ride a motorcycle to the mountains with a shiny fowling piece across his back and hunt pheasants every weekend?

One afternoon Tong came into the league's headquarters and announced excitedly to the vice-director, Jiao Luming, and several other men, "We got Li Thousand this time."

He put on the table a white paper ball and began unwrapping it. Then a broken Mao button emerged in front of them. They were shocked to see the Chairman's neck severed from his smiling face. "Where did you get this?" Jiao asked in surprise.

"Li Thousand dumped it into the trash heap near Victory Restaurant. I saw him do it with my own eyes," Tong said proudly.

This was a hideous crime. They decided to denounce Li Wan that very evening.

Li left work late that day after treating an injured stonecutter at the clinic. Six men were waiting for him before his house. The moment he appeared at the street corner, they went up to him, saying, "We are here to take you to a meeting."

"What meeting?" Li licked his upper lip.

"A denunciation meeting for you."

"For me? I'm not a reactionary element, am I?"

"Of course you are. Stop pretending. We all know you smashed the button of Chairman Mao."

"No, I didn't! It's made of porcelain. Dropped to the cement floor by accident."

It was no use arguing. They grabbed him and brought him to Carter Inn, where the league's headquarters was. With an upright body, I'm not scared of a slant shadow, Li thought. He had seen actions in the army and knew a few top leaders in the province. Why should he be afraid of this troop of shrimps and crabs? So he followed them calmly and even smoked a self-rolled cigarette on the way.

They brought him into the dining room, where about a hundred people were waiting. In the storm of slogans Li was taken to the front and was made to wear a placard that carried the large words in black ink: "Current Counterrevolutionary."

The director of the league, Lin Shou, announced, "Comrades, we found this in a trash heap today." He raised the broken button. "Criminal Li Wan committed the crime. He must have hated our Great Leader all the time."

"Down with counterrevolutionary Li Thousand," a middle-aged woman shouted in the crowd, and people followed her and raised their fists. They realized Li differed from them not only in wealth but also in outlook. This further convinced them of his wickedness.

But Li was not easily frightened. He gave them a contemptuous smile and said loudly, "You called me a counterrevolutionary? What a joke. When I risked my life fighting the American ghosts in Korea, where were you? What have you contributed to our country and the Party? Let me tell you, I was awarded a merit citation twice. With these hands I've saved hundreds of revolutionaries, who are still my friends." He threw up his hands that looked like a pair of small fans.

"'Don't rest on past glory, make new contributions,'" someone cried out, quoting Chairman Mao.

"Take this." Jiao slapped Li on the face and said through his teeth, "Go on bragging, I'll crack your skull. Damn you. You're a current landlord."

"Down with current landlord Li Wan," a man shouted, and the crowd followed him, shouting in unison.

Li was stunned by the slapping and the new phrase which he had never heard before, and he kept his Mongolian eyes low. Yet he managed to say, "I'm not a criminal. It was an accident. I wore the button when I was at work. It fell to the cement floor by itself as I was washing my hands."

"Who saw it?" Lin asked.

"Nobody, but I swear on my Party membership that every word I said is true."

"No, he's lying," several people said. Li's calm voice enraged them. Under such a circumstance another man would drop to his knees and beg for mercy, but Li, who had never been to a denunciation, had no idea of the propriety.

Then four men came in with long cudgels and ropes in their hands. They moved to the front and stood on both sides. "Will you admit your crime or not?" Jiao asked.

Though frightened, Li said, "I've nothing to admit. I love Chairman Mao and would sacrifice my life for him. How could I hate him? He saved my clan. My parents and grandparents all worked for landlords as farmhands. He is our Great Savior! How could I hate him?"

"Stop pretending," Director Lin cried. "Facts speak louder than words. Show us how you love Chairman Mao, damn you."

"Yes, show us."

"Show us how."

At once the room turned quiet, all eyes fixed on Li's fat face, as if they were waiting for him to sing a passionate song, or enact a Loyalty Dance, or do anything that could display that lofty feeling. Outside, a horse started neighing and drummed its hooves on the ground.

Li straightened up a little and smiled. Clearing his throat, he said, "All right, let me tell you something. Four years ago I mailed some food coupons, fifty kilos all together, to Chairman Mao. You all starved in the famine, didn't you? Me too. But unlike you, I ate a few mouthfuls less at every meal and saved the food coupons for Chairman Mao. Because I love him and didn't want him to starve like us. This was absolutely true. You can check it with my former army unit. If one word is untrue, behead me."

The crowd was thrown into a turmoil. Many of them couldn't help laughing, saying what an idiot Li was and how come he had thought Chairman Mao needed his food coupons, but nobody would say he didn't love the Chairman. The leaders of the league were confused by the sudden quirk, too, and they couldn't stop chuckling.

"Be quiet. Attention please," Director Lin shouted through his hands encircling his mouth.

To the crowd's surprise, Hou Mengtian, a young teacher in the Middle School, went up to the front. At the sight of this short man in glasses, Li quivered, because he remembered that this man had once wanted to borrow his German camera, but he had refused his request. Hou turned to the audience and said, "Don't be taken in by him. That's also a counterrevolutionary act." He turned to Li. "You think you're mighty smart and nobody can see through you, don't you? It's obvious that you sent the coupons to blaspheme Chairman Mao. You meant to say to him, 'Look, we are all starving because of your leadership.'"

"No," Li yelled, "I starved because I loved Chairman Mao!"

"See, how he used the words?" Hou said to the crowd. "He's blaming Chairman Mao. He starved because he loved Chairman Mao. If he hadn't loved him, he wouldn't have starved."

People remained silent, their faces showing confusion and eagerness. "Damn you, egg of a turtle!" Li cursed the young man.

"Watch your filthy mouth," Tong Fei cried.

"I can prove my point," Hou spoke again. "Four years ago he mailed the coupons, then the next year he came here. He thought the leaders in Beijing couldn't understand his trick? They saw through him. That's why he, a doctor with the rank of a captain, was discharged and sent here working in our small clinic."

Li looked blank and began trembling. It was as though he were hit on the head by a hammer, too dazed to respond to what was going on. Tears trickled down his cheeks.

"Comrades . . ." Hou spoke more confidently. "I suggest that we send someone to his army unit to find out the truth."

"Oh, we were told Chairman Mao had the same ration! Oh, oh," Li moaned and burst out sobbing, too overwhelmed to say anything clearly. People were finally convinced that he was indeed a wolf in human skin. Slogans and curses surged one after another. The men with cudgels fell on him.

"Oh, spare my life, ouch! I'm a counterrevolutionary, all right. Don't beat me!"

"Beat him!"

"Skin him!"

That night Li was jailed in the stable behind the inn, and a group of men went to his home and confiscated all the valuables and his bankbook. From the next day on, the motorcycle and the camera became public property and everybody in the league could use them (that was how dozens of men learned to ride a motorcycle); the fowling piece was committed to the care of the league's armed platoon. Of course, many of them enjoyed firing it when hunting pheasants and hares in the mountains.

A month later Li Wan was sent to Sea Nest Village to be re-formed. Lucky for him, he didn't labor in the fields. He served as a barefoot doctor there for five years, but without being paid. In the meantime, he wrote over a hundred letters to the Provincial Administration and Shenyang Military Region, asking for rehabilitation.

In the beginning of the sixth year his case was finally clarified. Flighty as he had been, he was by no means a counterrevolutionary. He was called back from the village. All the confiscated property was returned to him, but the motorcycle was already worn out and wouldn't start, the camera's lens was missing, and one of the barrels of the fowling piece had been blasted. Yet he got richer, because the bankbook was given back to him; in addition, he received a large sum of salary for his five years' work in the village. All at once his savings doubled. On the very day when he deposited the money in the People's Bank, the clerks there began spreading the news in town. Within a week, Li's nickname was changed to Ten Thousand, of which he seemed to be proud. How unjust the Lord of Heaven was! Li became the richest man again. Just the interest was more than a worker could make. This is exploitation, isn't it? everyone wondered.

Li simply despised the whole town, unable to get along with anybody. He bought a new motorcycle and a new camera, which was made in Shanghai, though. He had given up hunting but taken to fishing, so he bought himself two steel fishing poles and a large nylon net. These days he was thinking of buying a rubber boat. Still he wouldn't lend the camera to anyone; still he would give nobody a ride; still he would haggle with vendors in the marketplace and with hawkers on the streets. People went on talking about his stinginess and arrogance. In secret, some were looking forward to another political movement.

■ New Arrival

For years Jia Cheng thought of leaving his wife and starting a new family. When he bought her out of a brothel in Gold County eighteen years before, he had not expected she would be sterile, although she had told him about her numerous abortions and miscarriages during the years of prostitution and had mentioned her doubt about her fertility. She was a tall, handsome woman with smooth white skin, glossy dark hair, and long eyes, which together with the curved brows made her oval face rather graceful.

In the beginning Jia was happy, since his wife knew men well and tried to please him in many ways. She did everything out of gratitude. Because he had bought her out and given her a family, she hadn't had to stay in that profession any longer, to catch the pox and to be educated later in one of the schools set up by the communists to help and reform prostitutes from the old days. Nonetheless, she had been in three brothels for over ten years from the age of fourteen, long enough to forget her original name, which she probably had never had. A prostitute was always given a professional name, such as Spring Lotus, Gold Peony, Water Daffodil, White Dove. Usually the name changed once the woman was sold to another house. On the day when Jia bought his wife out, she signed as Ning Feng Wen—those words were the family names of the madams of the three brothels she had been through. From then on, that became her name.

Eighteen years passed. Jia was in his late fifties now, still working in the only photo shop in Dismount Fort. Year after year he expected to have a child, a son, but Ning had never been pregnant. Very often Jia regretted paying two hundred silver dollars for his wife. If he had known she was infertile, he would have chosen another woman. It serves you right, he thought. When you were young you only liked women who had kung fu in bed, but you didn't want to spend money visiting those pleasure houses every week, so you brought her home. Now it's too late to think of carrying on your family line. You're already an old useless dog. It serves you right.

"Did you touch the melons?" he asked his wife one Saturday afternoon.

"No, who wants to touch your rotten melons?" she said, knowing that he had hidden them away so as to take them to his mistress in Gold County the next morning.

"But two are missing," he said calmly.

"Where did you put them?"

"In the backyard."

"Probably a dog stole them," she answered without turning her head. She was busy making corn-flour porridge, beating the glue in a large bowl with an aluminum spoon.

Quietly Jia put the six remaining melons into a white cloth sack and carried them into the small dark room used for developing photographs.

Ning never asked him where he went on Sundays, but she knew, and tried hard not to let it disturb her. She had met hundreds of men. They were all the same and couldn't live without chasing a woman, just as every cat eats fish. She kept reminding herself that she mustn't stop Jia, who was her benefactor. Besides, she had promised him before their marriage that she would never interfere if he took another woman, and that she would remain his servant forever. Because the new government had banned polygamy, he couldn't have another wife, even though Ning was barren; in secret, however, he had been seeing another woman, whose name Ning didn't know. While she appeared composed, Ning was actually ill at ease. What if he gets a child with that woman? she thought. Will he walk out on me? Then, how can I live? Sometimes she woke at night, listening to the man snoring away beside her. She wanted to cry, but tears had stopped coming to her eyes long before. She thought it would have been better if she had never been born.

That evening after dinner, Aunt Zhang living on Eternal Way came to the Jias'. She sat on the edge of the brick bed, waving a palm-leaf fan. "Ning, do you want to make some money?" she asked.

"How?" Ning said, pouring Aunt Zhang a cup of boiled water.

"A young couple in the barracks are looking for a family to care for their baby boy. Sixteen yuan a month. They'll pay for all expenses." Aunt Zhang pressed Ning's white wrist with her shrunken hand as though to convince her that it was a good bargain.

"Well . . ." Ning paused. She had never done that kind of work before, but on second thought she felt like having a try. I can't always depend on my husband, she reasoned. If he runs out on me, I must make a living by myself.

"If you want to do it, tell me now," Aunt Zhang said. "The couple are desperate, because the officer is leaving for Great

Gourd Island in two days and the mother can't take care of the baby while working in the city. I'm sure lots of people will jump at the deal."

"All right, wait a minute, let me talk to Old Jia." Ning got up and went into the small dark room, where Jia was writing captions on photographs.

After a short while she reappeared and told Aunt Zhang that she would accept the work. As arranged, the young couple were to bring their two-year-old here the next morning.

"What's your name?" Ning asked the little boy.

"Tell Aunt your name," his mother said. She was a small, delicate woman working as a singer in an opera troupe in Dalian City.

"Lei," the boy mumbled.

"That's a good name. Would you like to have this, Lei?" Ning asked, leaning forward and showing him a toy duck with four wheels and a rope.

"Yeah," he said as he took the toy and put it on the floor. The wooden duck began quacking and flapping its wings while Lei drew it about the room.

He pulled too hard and overturned the duck, whose four wheels were speeding in the air. Immediately Ning squatted down and put the duck back on its feet. "Here you go, Lei," she said and touched his ruddy cheek. The duck resumed quacking.

While talking with the boy's father, a tall officer, Jia turned to watch the boy and the duck again and again. He was glad to see the little fellow so at ease. "He's a husky boy," he said to the young man, who had one stripe and four stars on his collar insignia. "You're lucky to have him."

"Sometimes he can be naughty. Don't spoil him," the officer said with a smile, then motioned to his son. "Come here, Little Lei, and meet your uncle."

The boy dragged the duck over and stopped in front of the men. "Call him Uncle Jia," his father told him.

"Ungle," he mumbled, then turned away with the duck quacking.

Jia was very pleased and took a melon out of the sack, which he had just put on a chair and was about to take with him for the ten o'clock train. He called the boy back. "Little Lei, would you like to have this?"

The boy's dark eyes stared at the melon and then at Jia. It seemed that he had never seen such a thing and was wondering whether it was something to play with or to eat.

"Don't give him that now," Ning said. "I've made some egg curd for him. Put it aside. He'll have it after the meal."

Jia put the melon on the table. Out of hospitality, he took another two from the sack for Lei's parents. "Try a melon please. They're very sweet," he said to them. His smile revealed a gold tooth. He was so excited that his long, leathery face turned a little pink, and he couldn't close his mouth to keep from smiling. His wife thought he looked silly.

The couple thanked him. Ning put two of the melons in a basin and washed them. Jia couldn't remain for long, since he had to catch the train. He excused himself, saying he had work to do, took up the partly empty sack, and left for the station.

"Lei, do you want to stay here or come with me?" Lei's mother asked, testing the boy. Her large eyes were winking at the young captain.

Lei looked at her, then muttered, "Stay."

"Good," his father said and laughed, "you're a brave boy. Mom and I will come to see you soon."

"Always listen to Aunt and Uncle, all right?" his mother said.

"Uh-huh." Lei nodded.

"He's like a big boy," Ning praised.

"We were afraid he wouldn't stay," the woman said to Ning. "I'm so glad he likes to be here." Her permed hair tilted a little toward the boy.

After they had tried the melons, Lei's parents left. Ning began to feed Lei egg curd and rice porridge. He had a good appetite, and his small mouth twitched with relish while he was chewing. Ning noticed he had eight teeth.

Gold County was thirty kilometers away from Dismount Fort, and four passenger trains went there every day. Jia returned before dinner, but he looked unhappy and kept himself in his dark room, sucking on a thick pipe. Through the opening between the window curtains, he saw Lei chasing chicks in the backyard. Meanwhile his wife was cooking dinner, the cornstalks sputtering under the cauldron.

Women are all greedy, he thought of his meeting with his mistress. Her face was long. "Three melons! Shame on you." No use to explain. She wouldn't try to understand. I bought eight originally, she didn't believe it. "You're so tight. I've never met a man like you." How many men has she met then? A hundred? For things to eat and wear, and for money? I didn't go whoring and didn't plan to pay. It was good that I had no money in my wallet today, or I'd have to give her some, to calm her down with a large bill. Never seen her so mad. Greedy, so greedy. Women're all the same. Waiting for me to bring her good stuff. At last she showed her true nature. Is she tired of me? Wants to get rid of me? Old, I'm old. So hard to please a woman.

Remember to bring her more stuff next week to make up for the three melons. What should I buy? A box of vanishing cream? No, I gave her one last month. A pair of nylon socks? What color does she like? No idea. How about some walnut cookies? Don't know. I'm tired. So ridiculous, like playing house with a small girl. You can't reason with a woman. She's well over forty and has married four times—

The door curtain opened. "Come out and eat," his wife said.

Jia emptied the pipe and went to the dining table. Already Lei was on the brick bed, trying to touch the white buns steaming on the low table in front of him. Ning moved to feed him rice and stewed sole. She gave him a cork, with which he was playing while eating.

The boy saw the roasted peanuts prepared for Jia's drink. He pointed his hooked finger at the peanuts and whined, "Waunt."

"Want this?" Jia asked, raising the whole dish.

"Don't give him that," his wife said. "Too young to chew."

"Waunt," Lei whined again.

"All right, take this spoon first." Ning put the rice into his mouth, picked up two peanuts, and started chewing.

In a few seconds she spat out a lump of peanut butter and placed it on the boy's pointed, waiting tongue. He swallowed the peanut butter and raised his eyes to look at Ning, then pointed at the peanuts and again whined, "Waunt." He gave a smile to Jia, who was drinking white spirits.

"Isn't Uncle's home good?" Jia asked.

"Goooood." Lei smiled, nodding his round head.

Ning chewed peanuts for him continuously while feeding him. Jia was pleased to watch his wife working with Lei. He took a sip of the liquor and said to Ning, "I like this boy a lot. He's so at home." He turned to Lei and said, "With a thick face, you can eat well everywhere in the world. Little Lei, do you have a thick face?"

"Yeah," the boy said out loud, pushing the spoon a little with his cheek.

"Don't talk with him," Ning complained. "Don't you see I'm busy feeding him?"

Lei's small eyes rested on the porcelain liquor pot. As Ning turned to refill the bowl, Lei raised his finger at the pot and whined again, "Waunt."

"Hey, he wants a drink," Jia cried.

"Don't give it to him. Too young for that stuff."

The boy understood her words, and his face began to change, his mouth spreading sideways as if he were about to burst into tears.

"All right, all right, Uncle let you try. She's bad," Jia coaxed and moved over with his cup. He dipped a chopstick into the liquor and then put a drop on the boy's tongue.

"Good?" Jia asked.

"Yeah." The boy smacked his lips and held out his tongue again.

"My, my, what a drinker. One more?" He gave Lei another drop.

"Don't give him too much. He'll get drunk."

Jia turned to move away, but the boy broke into a cry, kicking and screaming. Several flesh rings appeared on his short plump legs, and tears trickled down his chubby cheeks. Jia turned back and gave him a few drops more.

After supper Lei ran wild. His face was like a red apple, shining with happiness. He laughed loudly and played hide-and-seek with pillows on the large bed. Both Jia and his wife worried, fearing that the boy was too excited and might fall ill. They tried to make him go to bed, but he wanted to play more and even managed to get on Jia's neck for a horse ride. Not until ten o'clock did he agree to lie down between Ning and Jia. Lei slept so well that he wet the bed and didn't make any noise while Ning was carrying him to the chamber pot.

The following day at dinner Lei again wanted to drink from Jia's cup. Liquor was too strong for him, so Jia poured some apple wine into a cup that was as tiny as the bowl of a pipe. Lei liked the wine better because it tasted sweet. Every day he drank a cup and soon became Jia's wine buddy. Jia would smile and say, "Little Lei, you're lucky, Uncle have money and can buy you wine."

"Yeah," the boy would reply.

Sunday came. Jia had not yet decided whether to go to his mistress. During the day he was busy shooting and developing pictures at the photo shop, and in the evening he spent a lot of time playing with Lei, so he had forgotten to think of what gift he should take to the woman. Now he felt at a loss wondering if he had to see her so soon.

After breakfast he made up his mind not to go. Instead, he took the boy to the country fair. Swaying rhythmically with Lei on his back, Jia turned into Main Street and walked to the marketplace. Near the entrance of the army's clinic he met Meng

Long, the head of the town's slaughterhouse, who was sitting on a rock and basking in the sun. Meng rose to his feet and asked, "Who's this, Old Jia? A nephew or a relative?"

"A little friend," Jia said, smiling awkwardly. "His father is on Great Gourd Island, so he stays with us."

"Little fella, how old are you?"

"Dwo."

"He's big for two," Meng said, and patted Lei on the back.

"Yes, he's a good boy. We've got to go to the fair, Old Meng." Jia turned to Lei and said, "Say goodbye to Uncle Meng."

"Bye." The boy's white fist wheeled back and forth like a fat mushroom.

On such a fine summer day the fair was always crowded. The peasants from nearby villages were eager to sell their produce to get cash for groceries, which they could buy at the same place. Many kinds of craftsmen gathered here too: cobblers, blacksmiths, tailors, locksmiths, tinkers, knife grinders. Jia didn't want to buy anything, and he merely walked about and asked prices, comparing them with those of the year before.

"How much for an egg?"

"Seven fen. Buy some, Uncle."

"No, no." He continued to walk.

"What's the price for the crabs?" he asked, passing a fish stand.

"Ten for a yuan. Buy a dozen or two, Uncle Jia. They're fresh, caught this morning," the young vendor said.

"No, they're dead already."

Many people in the country knew Jia, for he was the most experienced photographer in the commune. Whenever they wanted to have a family picture taken, they went to his photo shop.

Jia noticed that quite a few young women he had never seen before carried baskets filled with vegetables, fruits, eggs, meat. They must have been the wives of some officers transferred to the Garrison Division recently. Most of the women were pretty and dressed well, and they didn't take the trouble to haggle. A slim young woman passed by with tomatoes in her basket, leaving behind a whiff of perfume that smelled of fresh apricot. Jia was wondering whether he should ask one or two of the young wives to sit for a large sample picture.

"Egg, egg," Lei sang in a small voice.

Jia turned around but saw no eggs. Then, following Lei's finger, he found a pile of potatoes on the ground. He couldn't help laughing.

The young vendor raised a potato and asked, "Little brother, you say this is an egg?"

"Egg, egg," Lei chanted as if to himself.

All the grown-ups around laughed. Jia explained, "He has never seen that."

"How about this?" a middle-aged man asked and showed Lei a large tomato.

"Egg, red egg."

People laughed again and the crowd was getting larger.

"My goodness, everything round is an egg," a young woman said loudly, and took a small pumpkin out of a gunnysack. "How do you call this, boy?"

"Egg, big egg."

The burst of laughter bewildered Lei, who looked at Jia in silence. "Stop teasing him," Jia shouted at the grown-ups. "He's not a monkey. What's so funny? Did you call everything right when you were just out of your mother's belly?"

Hurriedly he carried Lei away to a wall at the roadside and put him to the ground. "Those are not eggs, Lei," he said. "They're potatoes and tomatoes. The biggest one is called a pumpkin."

The boy stared at Jia with tearful eyes and puckered up his lips. He closed his eyes, crinkled his nose, and was about to cry. "All right, all right," Jia said and took him into his arms, "it's Uncle's fault. I didn't tell you their names beforehand. Don't cry. Lei's a good boy. Let me buy you a popsicle."

Lei also saw the old woman pushing a popsicle cart over, so Jia's words calmed him. Jia handed a five-fen coin to the woman and said, "One, please."

"Milk or red bean?"

"Milk."

Lei was sucking the popsicle. With amusement Jia watched him moving the ice around his mouth clumsily. He didn't try to help him, for fear Lei would be upset again. Let him enjoy himself that way. "Good?" he asked.

"Yeah." Lei stuck out his tongue, licking his lips.

Carrying the boy in his arms, Jia was making his way through the crowd back to the entrance of the market. Piglets screamed and cocks crowed, while butchers were chopping pork noisily at meat stands. A group of children surrounded an old deaf-mute woman who was using her fingers to bargain with an egg vendor. Beside the stand of jellied bean curd some old men sat on benches drinking tea and playing chess. In the shade of elms and locusts a few youngsters were reading picture-stories they rented from a bookstand. It was getting hot, and Jia began to sweat.

"Fresh jellyfish, ten fen a bowl," an old woman cried.

"Lei, let's have some jellyfish, all right?" Jia said.

The boy nodded. They went over and sat down at the stand. Jia bought a large bowl and a small bowl of sliced jellyfish spiced with parsley, leeks, and sesame oil. He started eating, while Lei would do nothing with the dish but stir it with a pair of chopsticks. Jia picked a piece of jellyfish from his own bowl and inserted it into Lei's mouth. The boy spat it out immediately.

"Don't like it?" asked Jia.

"Nah." Lei went on drumming the table with the chopsticks.

"Kids don't like jellyfish in the beginning," the woman said. "By and by they'll get used to it."

"Ha, you two are here." Ning emerged from behind, carrying a basket of eggplants and green beans. "I've looked everywhere and couldn't find you. Why did you stay so long? Is he all right?" she asked, pointing at Lei.

"He's fine," Jia said with a grin. "He likes looking around with me."

"Let's go home. It's getting too hot," Ning said, and picked up the boy and kissed him on the milky lips.

"Let me carry him." Jia got up.

His wife put the child on his back. She had bound feet, and the vegetables were heavy enough for her. Together they were walking back. On the way home they never stopped talking to the child, asking him questions and teaching him to name things. Ning remembered that her husband and she had not walked together on the street for at least nine or ten years. He always felt embarrassed walking with me, she thought. How happy he looks now, and even younger. This boy is a little devil and has caught his old heart. If only I could give him a child. He likes a house full of children and grandchildren. Too late. He should have married another woman.

Lei's mother came every other week and took him to their apartment in the army compound for a day, but his father couldn't return from the island so often. Strange to say, the son didn't miss his parents at all and was always happy when he was back with the Jias again. His mother was glad that he didn't cry when she left.

For two days Lei had a fever. Jia took him to Dr. Liu on Bath Street and brought back two packets of herbs. The doctor said there was too much fire in the boy—the Yang was too strong—so the medicine was to reduce the fire and build up the Yin. Ning decocted the herbs, but the boy disliked the bitter liquid. It took a lot of white sugar and sweet words to coax him into taking the medicine. Even so, the fever continued and Lei began to have a cough.

"Close up the mosquito curtain," Jia told his wife when she laid the sleeping boy on the bed. Behind Lei's ear they had found a red blotch, probably a mosquito bite.

"Don't you see I'm doing it?" She placed a pillow to hold down the opening of the curtain, then bent down and kissed the boy's cheek. "Little devil, you get better tomorrow," she said.

Jia turned off the light. It was sultry, so he took off his undershirt and underpants and lay down and closed his eyes. Lei's stuffy nose was whistling away softly in the dark. Soon Jia went to sleep.

At about one o'clock Ning's voice woke him up. "My old man, turn on the light. Lei's burning hot."

Jia pulled the lamp cord and sat up to have a look at the boy. He was terrified to find Lei's face covered with red spots. "My God, he has a rash!"

Ning climbed out of bed and went to the desk. She found an old thermometer in a drawer and brought it over. After shaking it down, she inserted it into the boy's armpit. "Lei, tell me where it hurts," she begged, tears coming to her eyes.

The boy moaned without answering. His lips were so parched they looked chafed. His jaw moved slightly as if chewing something. "Get some water for him," Ning told her husband.

Jia went into the kitchen and brought back a bowl of water, a spoon, and a wet towel. "Here, here you are," he said, and sat down by the child. "Lei, open your eyes. Can you see your uncle?" he asked.

The boy didn't respond. Ning took out the thermometer and raised it to the bulb. "Heavens! It reached the end!"

Jia grabbed the thermometer and read it. The mercury column passed 41 Centigrade. He jumped to his feet and took his undershirt, telling his wife, "You take care of him. I'm going to the clinic to get a doctor." He rushed out into the night.

He was running to the Commune Clinic, which was not far, just at the corner of Safe Street. A dog in a yard was roused by Jia's footsteps and started barking at him. He didn't bother to give it a look, and kept running and murmuring to himself, "Must save him. Must save him." The road of white gravel spread under his feet like a band of cloud in the moonlight. He didn't feel anything, as though flying to the street corner.

Within five minutes he arrived at the clinic and set about pounding the boards that covered the door and the windows, shouting, "Doctor, wake up and save life!"

He pounded and yelled for a while, but no response came from inside. He was wondering whether there was anyone on duty at all. Then it dawned on him to try the army's clinic. He turned around and dashed down Main Street.

The lights in the clinic were still on. Jia went directly to a screened window and saw a doctor and two nurses inside sterilizing something in a large boiling pot on an electric stove. He knocked at the windowsill. One of the women raised her head with a start. "What do you want in the middle of the night?" she asked. They all turned to gaze at the old man, who looked very pale and distracted.

"Help, doctor," Jia moaned. "My boy's dying."

"Why don't you go to the Commune Clinic?" the other nurse asked.

"Nobody's there. The boy is not mine. His father is an officer in your army. We look after the boy for him. Come and save his life, please!" Jia was choked with emotion, his deep-set eyes tearful. He wiped the sweat off his gray brows.

"All right, we're coming," the doctor said. He turned to one of the nurses, saying, "You stay here. Liang Fen and I are going with him."

They put on white robes, picked up a medical box and two flashlights, and went out. Jia rushed to the entrance to meet them.

The moment their shadows appeared at the front door, Jia ran up to them and with both hands he held the doctor's arm. "Thank you, young man. You've saved my old life. You're a good man. My wife and I—"

He stopped because Nurse Liang turned around, tittering.

"Look at yourself," the doctor said, laughing heartily. "You have nothing on below your waist, old man."

Jia looked down and saw himself without his underwear. "I— I—, too scared. Sorry, sorry," he mumbled, using his hands to cover himself.

The nurse took off her robe and handed it to Jia. "Put this on, Uncle," she said.

"Thanks, thanks." He wrapped himself up immediately.

They moved into the street and hurried east. Jia walked and ran continually while the doctor and the nurse were striding behind him. It was damp and foggy. Jia was fluttering along like a ghost in white on the street of the sleeping town.

Lei had measles. On hearing the diagnosis, both Jia and Ning felt relieved; they had thought it must have been something like smallpox. The nurse gave Lei an injection of penicillin, and the doctor, whose surname was Cui, told them not to worry about the rash, which would continue to spread over the boy's body but would disappear in a few days. The fever would go down every day, and a nurse would be assigned to come to give Lei the injection four times a day. In the meantime, they must let the boy rest well, drink more water, and eat liquid food.

When Dr. Cui and Nurse Liang were about to leave, Jia handed back the white robe and said with an awkward smile, "Thanks. I was so scared." He scratched his sparse hair.

"Next time, remember to wear your pants," the young man said and laughed. The nurse took back the robe, tittering.

After they left, Jia and Ning didn't go to bed. Instead they spent the small hours talking about the boy and watching his blotchy cheeks bulging out and sagging down, and they also rubbed him with a wet towel time and again. They smiled at each other, remembering how Lei had called the Moon Goddess on the wall his bride, how he had nodded his head when they asked him whether he would give them money when he grew up, how he had promised to give his mother a hundred yuan, his father a hundred, Ning a hundred, Jia a hundred, his Moon Bride a hundred, and himself a hundred, how he had wanted his picture-story books to be placed by his pillow when he went to bed, how he had passed water on the floor and cried heartbroken when Ning swept the mess away because he thought a small river of his was gone, how he had stepped on the feet of the baby boy of the Mings, then given him a candy when the boy was about to cry . . .

Beyond the windows roosters crowed, one after another. Dawn was approaching. How short was the night. They could have talked and talked for many more hours.

Three days later Lei's mother came to see him. He had almost recovered but still had brownish scales on the skin. She thanked the Jias for looking after Lei so well and then took him with her to spend the Sunday in their apartment. Though the Jias knew Lei would be back by the evening, they felt restless, as if they had not known where to put their own bodies. Jia didn't speak much, sitting in the backyard and pulling away on his pipe.

The day before, he had received a short letter from his mistress, who asked him to see her that Sunday. She said: "If you don't come this weekend, you mustn't see me again." Without much thinking, Jia wrote her a note which ended with these words: "I'm too busy on Sundays. Sorry, I cannot come. I really have no time. Too tired."

Aunt Zhang stopped by and chatted with Ning. She laughed when she heard Jia's night expedition to the army's clinic. "I have an idea," she said to the Jias. "Since you like the boy so much, why not take him as your nominal son? That will tie him to you forever, at least in name. I'm sure his parents won't mind. I can talk to them. That may make them feel more secure about leaving the boy with you."

Jia beamed and looked at his wife. Yes, why not?

But Ning frowned a little and said, "I've thought of that, Aunt Zhang. I don't think we should take Lei as a nominal son. You see, I'm an unlucky woman. If I'm fated to be childless, I shouldn't have one. Lei is a bright boy with a good future; I can't let my bad luck stand in his way and block his fortune. No, he's too good for us."

Aunt Zhang looked at Ning with amazement.

Jia stood up and walked away silently. He felt sad, but he believed Ning was right. The boy was too good to be their own. It was enough to know Lei would come back in the afternoon and to wait for him here when he stepped in. He would be happy if he could wait for him like this every Sunday. He knew that in a few years Lei would leave them for school in a bigger place and then go into the large world, but someday the boy might come back to this small town to see them, as a friend.

■ Emperor

We were playing horse ride in the afternoon on Main Street, which was a noncombat zone for the boys in Dismount Fort. The fourteen of us were in two groups. Seven were riding on the backs of the others, and we wouldn't switch roles until one rider's feet touched the ground. It was hot, though a breeze came now and then.

"Look at that," our emperor Benli said, pointing to a horse cart coming up the street. The harness bells jingled listlessly while the horses' hooves thudded on the white gravel. The cart was loaded with a mountain of beehives.

"Let's hit him," Bare Hips said. He referred to the cart driver, who looked tipsy and was humming a folk song.

Benli ordered, "Get ready."

We set about gathering stones and clods and hiding ourselves in the ditch along the road. About fifty paces behind us stood five latrine cleaners, resting in the shade of locusts. Ten buckets, filled with night soil, were reeking. Amused, the latrine cleaners watched us preparing to ambush the enemy's vehicle.

"Give me that brick, Grandson," Hare Lips said.

"No," Grandson said timidly, hiding the fragment of a brick behind him.

"Got a problem, eh? Refusing your grandpa?" Hare Lips slapped him on the face and grabbed the brick away from him.

Grandson didn't make a peep. He had another nickname, Big Babe, because he looked like a girl with curved brows, round eyes, a soft face, and a pair of plump hands with fleshy pits on the knuckles. He was too timid to fight anybody and every one of us could beat him easily. That was why he became our Grandson.

The cart was coming close, and the driver's voice was clear now:

> Square tables I ordered four,
> Long benches we have twelve,
> Meat and fish course by course,
> My brothers, help yourselves—

"Fire!" Benli shouted.

We started throwing stones, bricks, wooden grenades, and clods at the horses and the driver. He sat up with a start and turned his small egg-shaped face to us. Then he swung his long whip to urge the horses on. The lash was cracking like firecrackers while our missiles hit both the man and the horses, which were startled and began galloping. The latrine cleaners laughed noisily behind us.

Suddenly the whiplash touched the top of the load. A beehive tumbled down the other boxes, fell off the cart, and crashed to the ground. Bees poured out from all the hives. In a few seconds the cart was swathed by a golden cloud ringing madly.

"Oh Mother! Help!" the driver yelled.

The horses sprang up and plunged into the ditch on the other side of the road. The cart careened, turned over, and scattered the hives everywhere. Most of the bees were swarming to the struggling horses and the man; some were flying to us.

"Help! Help!" the driver screamed, but none of us dared move close. Even the latrine cleaners were too scared to go over, though one of them was running away to the Commune Clinic, which was nearby, to get help. Stunned, we dropped our weapons and watched speechlessly.

The three horses disentangled themselves and ran off with long neighing. The spotted shaft horse was charging toward us, and we all went behind the thick trees. It dashed by with a loud fart and kicked down two buckets of night soil. The street at once smelled like a compost heap.

"Help," the man groaned in the ditch, his voice very small. We couldn't see him. Over there only the swarm of bees was waving and rolling in the breeze.

Half an hour later most of the bees had flown away, and the medical people rescued the cart driver. He had stopped breathing, though we were told that his heart was still alive. His face was swollen, covered with blood and crushed bees, and his fingers looked like frozen carrots. They carried him on a stretcher, rushing back to the Commune Clinic.

Then Zu Ming, the head of town police, arrived and ordered everyone not to move, including the latrine cleaners. He must have heard that we had thrown things at the cart, for promptly he questioned us about who had started it. If we didn't tell him, he said, he would lock us up in the police station for a few days. We were scared.

"You," Zu pointed at Sickle Handle, "you hit a beehive with a stone, didn't you?" Zu's face was dark and long, so long that people called him Donkey Face.

"No, I didn't." Sickle Handle stepped away.

"How about you?" Zu pulled Benli's ear.

"No, not me." Our emperor grimaced, a thread of saliva dribbling from the corner of his mouth. "Oh, let me go, Uncle. It hurts."

"Then tell me who started it." Zu twisted Benli's ear harder.

"Ouch! Not me."

"Tell me who did it." A cigarette bobbed around the tip of Zu's nose as two lines of smoke dangled beneath his nostrils.

"He did it," Benli moaned.

"Who?"

"Grandson."

"Louder, I can't hear you."

"Grandson."

"Who is Grandson?" Zu let Benli go and looked around at us. Our eyes fell on Big Babe.

"No, I just threw one clod," Grandson said, his face turning pale.

"All right, one is enough. You come with me." Zu went up to Grandson, who was about to escape. Grandson had hardly run a step when Zu caught him by the neck. "You piglet, where are you going?" He threw him on his broad shoulder and carried him away to the police station.

"Fuck your mother!" Grandson yelled at Benli.

We all followed them to see what would happen to him, while the latrine cleaners laughed with their heads thrown back, pointing at Grandson, who was kicking in the air. Then they shouldered their loads of night soil and set out for Elm Village, where they lived. One of them carried two empty buckets with his pole.

"Stop it!" Zu whacked Grandson on the back, who stopped kicking instantly.

"Fuck all your grandmas!" Grandson shouted at us, wailing and sniffling.

We didn't swear back and followed them silently. The hot sun cast our slant shadows on the whitish road; cicadas were hissing tirelessly in the treetops. We hated Zu Ming, who only dared to bully us children. Two months ago he had gone to Dalian City with a truck from the Harvest Fertilizer Plant. There they had been caught by the gunfire of the revolutionary rebels. The driver, Squinty's father, was hit by a bullet in the leg, but he managed to drive the truck out of the city. Though nothing touched Zu, he was so frightened he messed his pants. The whole town knew that.

The blue door of the police station closed behind them. Bang, we heard Zu drop the boy on the floor.

"Oh! My arm," Grandson cried.

Immediately we rushed to the windows to watch. "Take this. I'm going to break your legs too." Zu kicked Grandson in the hips and stomach.

"Don't kick me!"

Two policemen came in, and Zu turned to them to explain what had happened. Fearing they might detain Grandson for some time and hurt him badly, Benli told Hare Lips, "Go tell his uncle that Big Babe is in trouble here."

Grandson's parents had died seven years before in a famine, so he lived at his uncle's. One reason we would make fun of him was that all his cousins were small girls. We could beat him or do him in without worrying about being caught by a bigger brother.

"Did you overeat, huh? Have too much energy?" Shen Li shouted, clutching Grandson's neck. Shen was a squat young man, like a Japanese soldier, so we called him Water Vat.

"Don't. You're hurting me!" Grandson cried.

"How about this?" A slap landed on his face.

"Oh!"

"Tell us why you did that."

"No, I didn't."

"You still don't admit it. All right, let your grandpa teach you how to be honest." Shen punched him in the flank.

"Ouch!" Grandson dropped to the floor, holding his sides and yelling, "Help! They're killing me."

"Shut up!" Zu ordered, and pulled him to his feet. "Now tell me, did you do it or not?"

Grandson nodded.

"Sign your name here then." Zu took him to a desk and pointed at a sheet of paper.

We were restless outside, having never seen how the police handled a child criminal. We were also anxious to get him out.

Finally Grandson's uncle came, wearing blue work clothes spattered with paint. We stepped aside to let the tall man go in. A few of us even ventured to enter together with him, but Water Vat pushed us back and shut the door.

We thought Grandson's uncle would be mad at the police, but to our surprise he cursed his nephew instead. "How many times did I tell you not to cause trouble on the streets, huh? Young rabbit, I'd better kill you or starve you to death." He slapped him on the face.

The policemen took both of them into another room. Since we couldn't see them anymore, we left the windowsills, cursing the police and their families. We swore we would whack Zu's oldest daughter once she started her first grade.

A few minutes later the door opened and Grandson and his uncle came out, the three policemen following behind. "Liu Bao," Zu said aloud, "keep a good eye on your boy. You see, that cart driver could have been killed. We don't want the youngster to commit homicide."

"I will, Chief Zu," Grandson's uncle said, then turned around and cursed under his breath, "Son of a bitch!" He gnashed his teeth, his wrinkled face ferocious.

Grandson had black eyes and swollen lips. His yellow T-shirt was stained with the blood from his nose. The red characters "Revolution to the End" became blurred on his chest. He was too deflated to swear anymore and only looked at us with his dim eyes.

His uncle took off his own straw hat and put it on Grandson's head. With his sinewy arm around his nephew's neck, the man led the boy home.

For a week Grandson didn't show up on the streets. During the day we played games—hitting bottle caps, fanning paper crackers, throwing knives, and waging cricket fights; in the evenings we gathered at the train station to make fun of strangers, calling them names or firing at them with slingshots. They could never catch us in the darkness. If they chased us we could easily throw them off, since they were not familiar with the streets and alleys. If they were women we would follow them and chant, "My little wife, come home with me. There's a warm bed and hot porridge." The women would stop to swear curses, which we always took with laughter.

In the meantime we had a big fight with the boys from Sand Village. They defeated us because they outnumbered us two to one. Also, their emperor, Hu Ba, was notorious for his ferocity. Most boys in town and its vicinity would slink away at the sight of him. On a victory, he would whip his captives with iron wire and even pee into their mouths. We were lucky, as we got captured and flogged but weren't humiliated further. They didn't catch our emperor, though, because Benli was a fast runner. They pursued him ten kilometers until he reached his aunt's home in Horse Village.

On the following Wednesday Grandson came out. To our amazement, all the bruises had disappeared from his face. He looked calm and was reticent, but his eyes were shining strangely.

That afternoon we had a clod fight in the backyard of the Middle School, where some sunken vegetable cellars could be used as trenches and strongholds. More clods were available there too, since no stones or any other hard things were allowed in a fight among friends. Emperor Benli divided us fourteen boys into two groups, one of which was to hold the eastern part of the yard while the other held the western part. The two groups would attack and counterattack until one side surrendered.

Bare Hips, Big Shrimp, Grandson, Squinty, and I and two smaller boys were to fight Benli, Hare Lips, Sickle Handle, and four other fellows. We collected clods and placed them on the edge of our trench, for we knew Benli's team was always on the offensive initially. We wanted to consume their ammunition first. Once they ran out of clods, we would fight them back to their trench and rout them there.

The fight started. As we expected, they began charging at us. Missiles were sailing over our heads while we were waiting patiently for them to come close. Our commander, Bare Hips, raised his hands, his fingers circling his eyes like binoculars, to observe the enemy approaching.

"Ready," he cried.

Every one of us held big clods like apples, preparing to give them the best of it. Bare Hips raised his left hand. "Fire!"

We all threw out clods, which stopped their charging immediately. One clod exploded on Hare Lips's head. With both hands around his skull, he fled back to their trench.

We jumped out to fight at close quarters. Seeing us fully equipped, they all turned around to escape, except Benli, who was still moving toward us. I hit him in the chest with a clod. It didn't stop him. Grandson hurled a big one at him, and it struck his head. "Oh!" Benli collapsed to the ground.

We laughed and ignored him, because he had been wiped out. We went on chasing the remnants. Hiding in the trench, they all saw their commander knocked down; since they had no ammunition left, we subdued them easily—one by one they raised their hands to surrender.

"Grandson, you ass ball!" Benli yelled behind us, and rushed over. "Fuck your grandma, you used stones." On his forehead a slant cut was bleeding. Blood trickled down around his left eye.

"So what?" Grandson said calmly. His voice startled us.

"Damn you, you took revenge." Benli moved forward, grabbing for him.

"Yes, I did." Grandson whipped out a dagger and waved it. "You touch me, I'll stab you through."

Benli froze, his hand covering his forehead. We dropped our clods and moved to separate them. Benli turned around to look for a stone while Grandson produced a cake of lead, which looked like a puck and was used in the game of hitting bottle caps. He raised it and declared, "I'm ready, Benli. You come close, I'll crush your skull with this." He looked pale, but his eyes were gleaming. "Come on, Benli," he said. "You have your parents at home. I don't have a mother. Let's kill each other and see who will lose more."

The emperor looked confused. We pushed him away and implored him not to further provoke Grandson, who was simply crazy and would do anything and could hurt anybody. We mustn't fight like this within our own camp.

"Enjoy picking apples at Willow Village, you bastard of a capitalist-backer," Grandson shouted at Benli. This was too much. Our emperor burst into tears. We knew his father had recently been removed from the Commune Administration for being a capitalist-backer and was going down to the countryside to reform himself through labor. The family was moving soon.

"Give me some paper, White Cat," Benli muttered to me. But I didn't have any paper with me.

"Here, here you are." Big Shrimp gave him an unfolded handbill.

Benli wiped the blood and sweat off his face and blew his stuffy nose. He couldn't stop his tears. We had never seen him cry like this before.

"Come on, let's go home," Bare Hips said. He took Benli's arm, and we started moving out of the yard.

Grandson was standing there alone in the scorching sun, as though he were not one of us. He chopped the lead in his hand with the dagger, watching us retreating; he spat to the ground and stamped on his own spittle.

After that fight, Grandson said he hated his nicknames and threatened to hit whoever happened to call him Grandson with the cake of lead, which he always carried with him. As for the other nickname, Big Babe, we had already dropped it of our own accord. In school, teachers called him Liu Damin, which was his real name but too formal to us street urchins. Only nicknames were acceptable among us. However, we found a solution to this problem. Benli was busy all the time helping his parents pack up and seldom played with us now, so we called Grandson "Vice-Emperor." And he seemed to like that name. To tell the truth, he wasn't a great fighter, but he was fierce and had more guts than the rest of us. Nobody among us dared challenge Emperor Benli and only Grandson could do it. Besides, he had been practicing with sandbags at night and had hard fists now. More important, after Benli's leaving we would have to choose a new emperor for our empire—the eastern part of town. Grandson seemed to be a natural candidate.

The day before Benli left we held a small party for him on top of a large haystack behind the Veterinary Station on the northern hill. Sickle Handle had lately stolen ten yuan from his father, who was a widower and a master blacksmith in the inn for carters and would get drunk at the end of the day. The old man couldn't keep track of his money, so his son always had a little cash on him and would share it with us. For the farewell party we bought sodas, boiled periwinkles, popsicles, moon cakes, toffees, melons, and haw jelly. Benli and Grandson were no longer on hostile terms, though they remained distant toward each other. We ate away, reminiscing about our victories over the enemies from different streets and villages and competing with each other in casting curses. A few golden butterflies and dragonflies were fluttering around us. The afternoon air was warm and clean, and the town below us seemed like a green harbor full of white sails.

Next morning we gathered at Benli's house to help load two horse carts. To our surprise, no adults showed up from the neighborhood, and we small boys could only carry a chair or a basin. Fortunately the two cart drivers were young and strong, so they helped move the big chests, cauldrons, and vegetable vats. Benli's father had seldom come out since he was named a capitalist-backer. We were amazed to find that his hair had turned gray in just two weeks. He looked downcast and his thick shoulders stooped. Throughout the moving he almost didn't say a word. Benli was quiet too, though his small brothers and sisters were noisy and often in our way. Before the carts departed, Benli's mother, a good woman, gave us each a large apple-pear.

After Benli left, the boys in the other parts of town attempted to invade our territory a few times, but we defeated them. To Grandson's credit, it must be said that he was an able emperor, relentless to the enemy and fair and square with his own men. Once we confiscated a pouch of coins from Red Rooster on Eternal Way, and Grandson distributed the money among us without taking a fen for himself. Another time we stole a crate of grapes from the army's grocery center; we all ate to our fill and took some home, but Grandson didn't take any back to his uncle's. Yet we couldn't help calling him Grandson occasionally, though nobody dared use that name in his presence. Because he held the throne firmly, the territorial order in town remained the same. No one could enter our streets without risking his skin. And of course we wouldn't transgress the borderlines either, unless it was necessary.

One afternoon we went shooting birds around the pig farm owned by the army. It was a stuffy day and we felt tired. For more than two hours the seven of us had killed only four sparrows. There weren't many birds to shoot at, so we decided to go and watch the butchers slaughtering pigs for the army's canteens and the officers' families. Then came Squinty, running over and panting hard. "Quick, let's go," he said, waving his hands. "Just now I saw Big Hat in town buying vinegar and soy sauce."

At once our spirit was aroused. Grandson told us to follow him to intercept Big Hat at the crossroads of Main Street and Blacksmith Road; then he ordered Squinty to run home and tell other boys to join us there. We set out running to the crossroads, waving our weapons and shouting, "Kill!"

Big Hat was the emperor of Green Village, whose boys we didn't know very well but fought with whenever we ran into them. He had gotten that nickname because he always wore a marten hat in winter and would brag that the hat made lots of big girls crazy about him. Usually he would come to town with two or three of his strong bodyguards, but today, according to Squinty's information, he was shopping here by himself. This inspired us to capture him. To subdue those country bandits, we had to catch their ringleader first.

No sooner had we arrived at the crossroads than Big Hat emerged down Blacksmith Road. He was walking stealthily under the eaves on the left side of the street, carrying on his back an empty manure basket and holding, in one hand, a long dung-fork and, in the other, a string bag of bottles. He looked taller than two months before when we had fought under White Stone Bridge near his village. Seeing us standing at the crossroads, he turned around. At this instant, Doggy and Squinty with a group of boys came out of the street corner and cut off Big Hat's retreat. Both units of our troops charged toward him, with sticks and stones in our hands. Knowing his doom, Big Hat stopped, put down the basket and the bottles, and stood with his back against the wall, holding the dung-fork.

"Put down your arms and we'll spare your life," Doggy cried. We surrounded him.

"Doggy," Big Hat said, "you son of a black-hearted rich peasant, don't stand in my way, or else we'll smash your old man's head next time he's paraded through our village." He grinned, and a star-shaped scar was revealed on his stubbly crown.

Doggy lowered his eyes and stopped moving. Indeed several weeks before, his father, a rich peasant in the old days, had been beaten in the marketplace during a denunciation. "Stop bluffing, you son of an ass!" Grandson shouted.

"Grandson," Big Hat said, "let me go just this once. My granduncle is waiting for me at home. We have guests today." He pointed at the squat bottle containing white spirits. "My granduncle is a sworn brother of Chairman Ding of our commune. If you let me go, I'll tell him to help promote your dad."

We all turned to look at Grandson. Apparently Big Hat thought Grandson's uncle was his father.

"Tell your granduncle we all fuck him and your grandaunt too!" Grandson said.

"Come on, your old man will be the head of his workshop if you let me go just this once. My granduncle is also a friend of Director Ma of the fertilizer plant."

"Fuck your granduncle!" Grandson plunged forward and hit Big Hat on the forehead with the cake of lead.

Big Hat dropped to the ground without making a noise, and the dung-fork sprang off and knocked down one of the bottles. Blood dripped on the front of his gray shirt. Between his eyebrows was a long clean cut as if inflicted by a knife. The air smelled of vinegar.

Big Hat was lying beneath the wall, his eyes shut and his mouth vomiting froth. We were scared and thought Grandson must have knocked him dead, but we dared not say a word.

A moment later Big Hat came to and began crying for help. Grandson went over and kicked him in the stomach. "Get up, you bum." He clutched his collar and pulled him up on his knees. "Today you met your grandpas. You must kowtow to everybody here and call us Grandpa, or you won't be able to go home tonight."

We were too shocked to do anything. "Grandson," Doggy tried to intervene, "spare his life, Grandson. Let him—"

"Stop calling me that!" Grandson yelled without looking at Doggy, then turned to Big Hat. "Do you want to call us Grandpa or not?"

"No." Tears covered Big Hat's face.

"All right." Grandson stepped away, picked up the fork, and smashed all the bottles. Dark soy sauce and colorless liquor splashed on the gravel and began fading away. "All right, if you don't, you must eat one of these." He pointed to the horse droppings a few paces away.

"No!"

"Eat the dung," Grandson ordered, and whacked Big Hat on the back with the fork.

"Oh, help!"

The street was unusually quiet, no grown-ups in sight. "Yes or no?" Grandson asked.

"No."

"Say it again."

"No!"

"Take this." Grandson stabbed him in the leg with the fork.

"Oh! Save my life!"

One of the prongs pierced Big Hat's calf. He was rolling on the ground, cursing, wailing, and yelling. Strangely enough, no grown-ups ever showed up.

This was too much. Surely we wanted to see that bastard's blood, but we wouldn't kill him and go to jail for that, so a few of us moved to stop Grandson.

"Keep back, all of you." He wielded the fork around as if he would strike any of us. We stood still.

Grandson picked up one of the droppings with the fork and raised it to Big Hat's lips. He threatened, "If you don't take a bite I'll gut you. Open your mouth."

"Oh! You bandit," Big Hat moaned with his eyes closed. His mouth opened a little.

"Open big," Grandson ordered, and thrust the dung into his mouth.

"Ah!" Big Hat spat it out and rubbed his lips with his sleeves. "Fuck your mother!" he yelled, and lay on his side wailing with both hands covering his face.

Grandson threw the fork to the other side of the street; he looked around at us with his crazed eyes, then walked away without a word. His broad hips and short legs swayed as though he were stamping and crushing something.

Without any delay we all ran away, leaving Big Hat to curse and weep alone.

Shortly afterward Grandson became famous. Boys of the lower grades in our Central Elementary School would tremble at the mere sight of him. With him leading us, we could enter some other areas of town without provoking a fight. Except for us, no one dared play on Main Street any longer—the former non-combat zone was under our control now. Some of the officers' children, a bunch of weaklings though they ate meat and white bread and wore better clothes, even begged us to protect them on their way to school and back home. They would pay us with tickets for the movies shown in the army's theater and with tofu coupons, since Sickle Handle's father, the old blacksmith, had lost all his teeth and liked soft food. For a short while our territory was expanding, our affairs were prosperous, and our Eastern Empire began to dominate Dismount Fort.

But a month later, Grandson's uncle failed to renew his contract and couldn't find work in town. We were surprised to hear that he hadn't been a permanent, but a temporary worker in the fertilizer plant. The Lius decided to return to their home village in Tile County.

Grandson left with the family, and our empire collapsed. Because none of us was suited to be an emperor, the throne remained unoccupied. Now boys from the south even dared to play horse ride in front of our former headquarters—Benli's house. We were unable to go to the department store at the western end of Main Street or to the marketplace to buy things for our parents and rent picture-story books. Most of us were beaten in school. Once I was caught by Big Hat's men at the millhouse and was forced to meow for them. How we missed our old glorious days!

As time went by, we left, one after another, to serve different emperors.

■ Fortune

Blind Bea, a locksmith, used to be a street fortune-teller in the old days. Though his practice was banned in the New China, people in Dismount Fort had never stopped seeing him in secret. Whenever there was a wedding or a funeral, they would go to him beforehand and ask about a lucky day or a good burial place. Because of his poor sight, Bea seldom went out, but he knew what was happening in town. Some people believed he was a kind of scholar who could fathom the mysteries between heaven and earth without stepping out of his threshold. Blind Bea lived well. Except for the children who often watched him through the back window of his hovel, nobody was jealous of his eating large white bread at lunch and dinner.

Tang Hu of Sand Village heard that a month ago a peasant had lost a horse and gone to the fortune-teller to ask its whereabouts. After reading the bamboo slips, Blind Bea raised his knotted hand and boomed out, "He carried his balls to the poplar woods in the east." The owner of the horse said it was a mare, but Bea told him to forget male or female and just go search the woods. A few men went there and found the horse.

These days Tang had been thinking of visiting Blind Bea, because he had been dogged by bad luck for the past few years. The summer before last he lost two litters of piglets, and last fall a flood ruined his cabbages and turnips. Then he had acute appendicitis and could have died if a truck hadn't happened to be passing the village and carried him to the Commune Clinic in time. Nonetheless, the doctors opened his stomach, and Tang lost all the original wind his parents had put in him. He wondered whether these misfortunes had been caused by the graves of his ancestors which faced east instead of south.

Tang pulled up his horse cart before the locksmith's and went inside. Blind Bea crouched over a vise filing the copper switch of a flashlight. At the sight of Tang he put down the rasp and returned to the armchair covered with a roe deer's skin.

"Take a seat," Bea said.

Tang sat down and explained what was on his mind. Blind Bea asked his name and the hour and date of his birth. Then he closed his eyes and sat back, mumbling something to himself while fingering a string of green-jade beads. Tang rolled up a cigarette and lit it. A dragonfly was fluttering on the wire gauze of the window, struggling in vain to get out.

"I don't see any problem here," Bea said three minutes later.

"Not because of my ancestors' graves?"

"No. According to the Diagram, you should have a mighty life. You were born to be a big general. Those graves can't stop you at all."

"Really?" Tang was surprised. "You say I'm going to be a general?"

"Maybe. Although the Diagram says you were born to decide

the life or death of thousands, it depends on whether you can realize your destiny."

Tang turned his head aside and thought for a moment. "Then how come I had bad luck these years?" he asked.

"Let's see. What's your son's name?"

"Da Long."

"What? A great dragon?"

"Yes."

Blind Bea shook his head and began leafing through a dog-eared book. He stopped at a page and read for a minute. "That won't do," he said.

"What won't do?"

"Your son's life is too strong. His fortune reduces yours, and he is the evil star over your head. 'Da Long,' what a name! Only a king should have such a name. The truth is that he is a dragon, while you're a tiger. His life has overcome yours. See, you're forty-three now. At your age lots of men have already made their fame and wealth, but you're still a cart driver, commanding only a couple of scabby horses." Blind Bea chuckled and lit his long pipe. Smoke came out through his yellow teeth.

"What should I do?" Tang asked.

"How old is your son?"

"Fourteen."

"Too late."

"What do you mean?"

"If he was under ten, you could change his name without hurting your fortune."

"But what am I to do now?"

"Have his name changed. It'll hurt, but it's better than do nothing about it."

Silence.

The two men seemed deliberately to avoid looking at each other. Then Tang said, "What name should he have?"

Bea opened a notebook, tore a page out, and handed it to Tang. His other hand removed the horn-rimmed glasses from his broad face, revealing eyes like a dead fish's.

Taking the paper, Tang lowered his head to read it. He found five bold characters in a vertical line: "Horse, Ox, Dog, Mountain, Spirit."

"Damn it," he cursed, and struck his thigh with a fist as thick as a horse hoof, his long eyes tilting up to his temples.

"You'd better hurry. There aren't many years left," Bea said absently. "A man over forty is like the day in the afternoon. You know that."

Tang Hu got up and produced a one-yuan bill. "Old Bea, I understand. Thank you for telling me the truth." He placed the money in Bea's hand and put on his straw hat. He turned to the door, whose frame seemed too low for his large body, and bent down to get out.

The horses were drawing a large load of rocks along Eternal Way in Dismount Fort, a small town that in the ancient times had been a transfer post where Chinese troops stopped for rest and preparation on their expeditions to Korea. It was a hot windless day, and all the windows of the houses on the street were open. Flies were buzzing around Tang and landed on the horses. At a street corner a grinder was chanting "Hone a knife and sharpen scissors."

Brandishing the whip once in a while, Tang was lost in thought and let the horses find the way home by themselves. From the moment of his birth, I knew he was a jinx to me, Tang thought. He never slept quietly at night, waking up every other hour, playing and crying. My wife had to take care of him day and night. He allowed nobody in the house to have a good sleep. A selfish brat from the beginning. . . . He shat on my neck. I never carried him again. Everybody in the village laughed at me. A son shat on his dad's neck. Son of a rabbit, he's been shitting on me all these years! . . . My fortune is going down day by day, while his fortune is growing like grass. In the first grade he was a group leader in the Young Pioneers; a year later, a bugler; then a brigade leader. Always got high grades. So many awards on the walls. Only fourteen, already attractive to girls. Orchid of the Lius comes to do homework with him three times a week in the evenings. A small womanizer, learning fast. No, a born one.

I never touched a woman until I was twenty-seven. No girls would look at me, because of my cross-eyes. They wouldn't think of me as a man, because I was poor and my folks were humble. Who knows I was born to be a general and would command thousands of men and horses? Do for their ancestors, they think me no more than a sheep that anyone can kick, a dumb ass that anyone can flog, a chamber pot that anyone can pee into. A caged tiger is a puny animal compared with a free dog. . . . Dragon boy, you're strong because you have a tiger dad, because I spilled the best of mine into your life. Cocky boy, you laughed at me because I misread the character "vicious" as "wolf." It served you right. Those slaps were a good lesson, to teach you to be filial. Young wolf, you've been eating away my fortune all these years. This time we must settle everything and you must change your name.

The cart entered Sand Village. The tall cypresses thrust themselves into Tang's field of vision. Cracking the whip, he hurried the horses to the construction site in the orchard to unload the rocks.

The sun had just gone down behind the western hill and cast on the woods and fields the vast shade that was gliding east rapidly. The chime for ceasing work was sent out from a yard of I-steel hung on an ancient elm outside the production brigade's office. Hearing the chime, the commune members wiped the blades of their sickles and hoes and began going home. Soon the winch at the well by the village entrance started squeaking, buckets were clanking on the streets, and bellows were burring in every house. A loudspeaker announced repeatedly that all newlyweds must attend a family-planning meeting at seven in the evening.

After dinner, Tang talked to his son about changing his name. His wife, Zhen, was stitching the sole of a cloth shoe, and Hsia, his daughter, lay prone on the brick bed reading a textbook on nature.

"No, I don't want to change my name," Da Long said.

"You must," Tang said. "From now on, you'll be called Horse."

"No, I'm not a horse! What a dumb name."

"All right, you're Ox."

"No, I'm not stupid like an ox. I'm smarter than the other boys at school."

"Don't be so arrogant. Chairman Mao says everyone should be a willing ox in serving the revolutionary cause. Don't you remember that?"

"My old man," Zhen put in, "why do you want to have his name changed all of a sudden?"

"His name is a jinx to me." Without waiting for a response, Tang turned to his son again. "It's an honor to be Ox."

"I don't want to be that. Everybody is used to my name already."

"Damn it, then from now on you are Dog."

"What a joke! All my classmates will make fun of me for such a name."

"All right, you're Mountain then."

"Why don't you call yourself Mountain?"

Tang stood up and went for his son. "Don't, please," Zhen begged, holding his arm.

"Dad," Hsia said and sat up, "you're too superstitious. We're in the New China now. Who would believe a name is a jinx?"

"Shut up, girl!" Again Tang turned to his son. "Da Long, now you must call yourself Spirit."

"Crazy." The boy shook his head. "I'm an atheist, a leader in the Young Pioneers. How can I call myself that?"

"The word 'Spirit' doesn't mean a god here," Tang said. "It's a good word and means the best of a man. Our family name, Tang, is the same word as the great dynasty's. See, with such a name you'll carry on the best of China's most glorious past. Isn't it good enough, Tang Spirit?"

"No, it sounds silly. I don't want to change my name."

"Are you my son or not?"

"Yes, I am. All right?"

"Then you must be filial and listen to me. In the old days, Hua Mulan was enlisted and went to battles for her dad. She was merely a young girl, but was willing to die for her dad. Now I don't ask you to shed a drop of blood for me, and I just want you to change a word in your name, but you refuse me. You're a vicious boy, a young wolf. Oh heaven, how come I have such a son? I curse the day when he was conceived!" Tang grasped the front of his own jacket.

"Such an old fogy," Da Long muttered.

Tang jumped up and struck his son on the crown. "Don't you ever talk back like that!"

The boy fell to the ground, covering his head with both hands. Tang kicked him in the rump. "Let me teach you how to behave," he said between his teeth.

Tears were trickling down Da Long's cheeks, and Hsia burst out crying. "My old man, please don't be so angry," Zhen said timidly.

Somewhat bewildered by his own act, Tang picked up his tobacco pouch and moved to the door.

"Come back, please," his wife begged. "Come back, my old man."

"I don't want to see the face of my disobedient son," Tang cried. Without turning his head, he walked into the twilight.

He was heading for the Green Snake Stream, brooding and smoking a thick cigarette rolled by himself. I shouldn't have beaten him like that, he thought. But he's bad, always talking back. . . . Yes, I was mad. Why do you hate him so much? I don't hate him. Just want him to change his name. There's no way to bring him around. An impossible boy. I brought him up, but he doesn't have a bit of sense of filial duty. Worse than a dog. I should've gotten rid of him when he was a baby. He's too big now.

Oddly enough, Tang remembered that once a boy in the neighborhood had struck Da Long in the head with a stone. He picked up his son and ran to the village's barefoot doctor. The sight of his son's bleeding hurt him so much that he couldn't suppress his own tears and held him tight against himself. At that time Da Long had been small and helpless, but now he was big and strong, ready to eat up his father's fortune like a wild dragon.

Tang lay down on the cool grass of the riverbank, watching stars flickering behind a misty curtain. It was quiet; now and then a frog jumped into the stream and a dog barked from the village. They say there are men on some of those stars, he thought. Why so many men? Men are beasts, have to stamp each other, bully each other, kill each other, eat each other. All the village leaders suck our marrow and drink our blood, don't they? The share of fortune is basically the same for everyone. Some people are better off because they've stolen others' shares. That was why we killed those landlords in the Land Reform. To get our shares back. Someday we'll have another movement like that and wipe out all the village leaders. We'll begin with Director Hu, that egg of a turtle. This morning he raised his forefinger the moment I begged him to have Da Long's name changed in the brigade's registration book. Damn his mother, a hundred yuan is half a year's income. Even if I had the money I wouldn't give him any. Someday we'll have him beheaded, after chopping off that crooked finger first.

Tang sighed and exhaled smoke. A wolf was howling on the other side of the river. He continued to think, I should've changed Da Long's name ten years ago. Too late. I can't keep him down now. I'm old, and can't even subdue my son. How can I command an army of men and horses? Too old to be a general, and don't have the strength to fight thousands of enemy anymore. . . . Then let him flourish? Let him grow into a big man? Are you going to give up? I'm too old to be his match. Maybe I should let him grow. Hope he'll treat me respectfully when he becomes a big man. It's unlikely, such a heartless boy.

The heavy dew made mosquitoes unable to fly, so that the air felt cooler and fresher. In the moonlight Tang lay by the stream flowing with tiny sparks until all noises faded away. He became rather calm after being alone for hours and decided to put the matter aside for the moment. He would consult Blind Bea again and see if there was an alternative.

Two days later Tang again went to the quarry to haul back rocks via Dismount Fort. On his way there, he stopped at the locksmith's and had his fortune re-examined. To his dismay, Blind Bea told him bluntly that there was no alternative. All he could do was have Da Long's name changed. Bea blinked his red eyes meaningfully and said, "You know what you should do when a bad son becomes incorrigible. What's the good of such a son, anyway?"

After leaving Bea, Tang tried not to think of his fate and his son's fortune, but Bea's voice kept ringing in his ears and enticing him to imagine the wealth, rank, splendor of his future. For over thirty years he had worked in the fields, watering the soil with his sweat, and he could eat white steamed-bread only three or four times a year on holidays. Life was unfair. Why did he have to drudge like a beast? He was not born a slave. Why didn't he deserve a change?

On his way back, as the cart was jolting down Blacksmith Road, Tang saw some children and adults hurrying to the headquarters of the Garrison Division. He felt strange, because usually civilians were not allowed to enter the barracks. He urged the horses on.

At the front entrance of the headquarters the iron gate was wide open. On the two concrete pillars were posted Chairman Mao's instruction in fresh ink: "The Army and the People Unite like One Man; Under Heaven Who Dares to Be Our Match!" Several teenage boys were hastening through the entrance, but the two armed sentries just let them pass as though the youngsters had been officers' family members. Inside the barracks a large crowd of both civilians and army men surrounded the basketball court before the four-story building. Tang realized a game was going on, but why were the civilians allowed to watch?

He stopped the cart at the roadside and tied the front horses to a thick aspen. "What's up there, son?" he asked a boy running by.

"The Provincial Team is playing the Military Region. Hurry, we all can go in and watch."

Following others, Tang went into the barracks, but unlike others, this was his first time. There were so many things he had never seen before: the well-kept ilex hedges, a pair of huge searchlights flashing in the sun, the tall aerials, the dark targets of human forms, the instruments for physical training. What impressed him most were a line of six howitzers pointing to the southern sky and five dark limousines parked along the red building. A dozen guards strolled around, toting submachine guns.

Tang elbowed his way through the crowd to the front where everyone had to sit down. On the opposite side, the scoreboard announced "76 : 72," in favor of the army. To Tang's surprise, on his right a small man in woolen uniform and a fat official in a blue Mao suit were sitting in rattan chairs by a long table covered with white cloth. On the table were glasses and plates of fruits and candies. The crowd was kept ten feet away from the two men. A young woman in full uniform was pouring tea for them.

"That's General Wang," someone whispered in the crowd.

Tang's eyes were riveted on the small man's shoulders that each carried three gold stars. A real general. But he was so thin and so small, in no way like those ancient generals radiating a tiger's spirit. Any man on the street could look more like a general than this one. Tang's eyes turned and fell on those young women soldiers and officers. He had never seen women wear army skirts, which gave fine lines to their bodies. These women were pretty and sturdy, every one of them. Look, that one stood up and handed a wet towel to the general. Tang was stunned, having never imagined a general had so many young wives. And every one of them was as good-looking as an actress in the movies. God knew how many husky, handsome sons they had given and would give that small man.

A woman in steel-rimmed glasses went over and whispered in the general's ear, while he was nodding his gray head and wiping his sunken mouth with the towel. After she left, the general took a cigarette out of a gold case, and another young woman struck a match for him immediately. How could such a scarecrow command the entire military region? Impossible. Even too old to satisfy his women. He was useless and should have been dismissed long ago.

The enchanted cart driver moved forward to take a better look at the general's face. Absentminded, he put his leg into the court. "Ouch!" he cried out, and almost jumped up.

A young officer had kicked Tang's leg, which withdrew from the court instantly. Tang turned to glare at the young man, his big eyes so ferocious that the officer was taken aback. "I will remember you, son of a bitch," Tang cursed under his breath.

The officer turned around to watch the game. From behind, Tang fixed his eyes on the man's cupped ears and then measured his height—five feet nine. One stripe with two stars. You wait, young cock, he thought. I'll have you raise pigs when I become a general. I'll remember you and will nab you. You have eyes, but they don't see your lord. I'll have one of them plucked out. I swear in the honor of my ancestors, who have the same name as the great dynasty, I will—

The ending whistle cut off Tang's thought. He turned his eyes to the general, who stood up and shook hands with the fat official. Then the young women moved with him toward the limousines. The woman carrying a medical box even held his arm to support him. Not many days left. He could hardly walk. It was time for a new general to take over.

Having watched the small man climb into the second limousine, Tang turned and retreated with the crowd to the front entrance. A warm breeze blew across his burning face; the scorching sun made the air flicker slightly. He felt as though he were an immortal, his feet stepping on the clouds and his eyes seeing a lot of stars and rainbows dancing on the horizon. Hope at last settled in his heart.

For several days Tang was thinking how to get rid of Da Long. He wouldn't knife or hammer him. That would demand so much from himself that he might not be able to carry it through. He imagined taking his son onto a mountain and pushing him down a cliff, but all the hills nearby were not high enough. How about drowning him? There was only one reservoir in the village, and the two men in charge of the pump house were on the site all the time. Besides, Da Long could do the doggy stroke. If he put him away, he had to do a clean job and make sure that everything looked natural. Yes, he had it. Electrocute him. But how? He didn't know how to handle electricity himself. It was too dangerous, and he might kill himself and others. Have some help? No, he had to do it by himself, no money for that.

Though never able to work out a perfect plan that would guarantee his son's death, Tang did make one. He decided to use the horse cart, which Da Long had been learning how to drive. It was too bad that no rocks were to be transported anymore; otherwise Tang could easily have had the cart overturned and the boy buried by a load of rocks. These days he hauled only crops from the fields to the threshing ground.

One afternoon before leaving for work, Tang picked a few tiny peppers from his garden and put them into his tobacco pouch. The country folk called that kind of pepper "dog penis" because it was extremely hot and also resembled that organ of a dog. Tang threw on the cart a rope and a large wooden peg used for tightening up a crop load, and then he set out with his son for the millet field on the northern hill. Da Long was driving.

Sitting side by side, they didn't speak on the way. Tang was smoking, and occasionally he squinted at his son. The boy was handsome: full forehead, thick brows, square mouth; so handsome that Tang wondered whether Da Long was his own son. Probably a wild seed, destined to be plucked off the soil. Then he felt a numb pain in his chest, and his head seemed to be reeling. I must do it, he said to himself. Without cruelty a man is nothing, just like a knife without steel in its blade. You have to sacrifice something to get another thing. He is taking away all my fortune. It's time to wind things up. There aren't many years left and I must do it now.

While several commune members were loading the cart and his son went into the cornfield to urinate, Tang approached the shaft horse quietly. He tapped its hindquarters and lifted its tail, then thrust a pepper into its anus. The horse quivered, but regained its calm manner as though nothing had happened. In the same way Tang fixed the other two horses.

A mountain of millet rose on the cart, and at the back of the load a man was turning the peg to tighten the rope. Da Long returned. His father walked over and handed him the whip, and said, "You drive it to the threshing ground. I have something to do in the field here."

"All right," the boy said, taking the whip. He had driven loads of crops before and didn't suspect anything.

Watching his son's triangular back, Tang realized the boy was almost a man. This further convinced him that he was doing a timely thing. Heaven help! Let it work out.

With a slight toss, the cart started moving out of the field. Everything seemed normal, and the other people turned to their work. Tang stood there, watching the load wavering toward the road and wondering why the hot peppers didn't work. The load of the crop sank and rose, bumped a little, and got onto the surface of the road. As soon as the cart wheeled around to move down the slope a front horse, the roan stallion, plunged. Then the other horses began galloping too. The load was jolting wildly from side to side.

"Help!" The boy's cry rent the air.

People were too shocked to respond at once. Without a word Tang was dashing toward the bumping cart. "Let's go help," someone shouted. Several men set off running behind Tang.

The load of the crop was plunging down the mountain road. The din of the horses' hooves, the wheels, and the boy's cries was fading away. After a few turns the cart disappeared; so did the noises, except for the horses' neighing. Tang was running desperately. Gasping hard for breath, he felt as though his head was going to explode. Sparks and golden rings were floating around him while a taste of blood surged up into his throat. The commune members, left far behind, were amazed by his speed.

The cart fell into a small valley. Millet bundles were scattered everywhere, a few hung on the branches of apple trees. There beside a wheel lay Da Long, his eyes shut and his lips puffing out scarlet froth. Blood was trickling out of his nostrils. Tang threw himself at his son's side and lifted his head up. The boy moaned, without much breath left in him. His chest had been crushed. Tears sprang to Tang's eyes. It dawned on him that there was no hope for his son anymore and that he'd better finish him off. He looked around but couldn't find a rock, then he saw the peg partly underneath a bundle. He picked it up, raised it with both hands, and struck Da Long on the skull.

"Hold it!" someone yelled from behind. "Don't do it, Uncle Tang!"

The voice startled Tang and the peg fell to the ground. His son stopped breathing instantly. Two men grabbed Tang while others carried the boy off to the village. Everybody blamed Tang for his bad temper. However angry he was with his son for the accident, Da Long was merely a fourteen-year-old and a new hand in the work; there was no reason for Tang to strike him like that.

Besides, the boy was dying, no father would beat a dying son. It was inhuman not to save the life in danger. Some people believed Tang had actually killed Da Long with the peg.

After the boy's burial Zhen, together with Hsia, left for her parents' in Apricot Village that very day. She couldn't bear to see her husband drink hard and eat fish and meat. He had even killed the only four chickens that the commune allowed the family to raise. Nobody understood why Tang enjoyed himself so much, sonless though he was now. In the meantime the whole village was talking about his bad temper and cruelty.

Next morning two Beijing jeeps pulled up before the Tangs', and a group of policemen jumped off and surrounded the yard. Two of them entered the front gate with pistols in their hands. Tang saw them and understood it was time to leave, so he put on an army cap and for the first time buckled his broad leather belt around his waist. He didn't bother to look at the police, whom he simply took as his bodyguards. In a few days they would all salute him as General Tang. Surprised by his calm appearance, the two policemen stepped aside and let him pass without handcuffing him. They followed him out.

Tang inhaled the fresh air that made his chest contract with joy. In the distance, colorful clouds were tumbling and gleaming on the treetops like an army of horses and men marching onto a battlefield. He stopped and narrowed his eyes, listening to a bugle call to charge, the beating of drums, the din of a hot battle, the shouts of killing, the sweet female voices singing triumphant songs, the clinking of glasses mixed with the tunes of pipes and strings, the hurrays for the grand general, the explosions of firecrackers, and salvos. He smelled the fragrance of gunpowder and roast pigs.

"Ha, ha, ha—ha—" he laughed heartily to the sky while striding to the jeep. Never had he felt more like a man.

■ Taking a Husband

The moment Hong Chen entered the narrow lane leading to Lilian's house, a bloody rooster landed before her, jumping about and scattering its feathers. Four little boys ran over with knives and a hatchet in their hands. "Kill, kill him!" one boy cried, but none of them dared approach the rooster, whose throat was cut half through.

Lilian's big body appeared; she was carrying a cleaver. "Finish him off, boys. Don't let him suffer!" she cried. She walked over and stamped the dancing rooster to the ground. The biggest boy raised the hatchet and chopped the dangling head off.

At the sight of Hong, Lilian took her foot off the rooster and said, "I'm helping them kill the chicken. Their parents shouldn't let these boys do this. It's crazy. Blood is everywhere."

"I can smell it," Hong said. Together they entered the house.

"My parents are not home." Lilian patted Hong's arm with her free hand. She stood the cleaver on a cutting board, on which was a pile of cabbage leaves that she had just chopped for the ducks. She washed her hands in a basin and then led Hong into her own room.

Without delay, Hong said Pang Hai's matchmaker had come to press her again. She asked Lilian whether there was any news about who would become the commune's vice-chairman. Lilian's father was a train attendant going to the county town three or four times a week, so he might learn the news before others.

"No, I haven't heard of anything." Lilian rolled her broad eyes.

"What should I do?" Hong sighed and placed her slender hands on her lap.

"If I were you, I'd take Pang Hai."

"Why?"

"We don't know which one of them will be the chairman, right? We can assume they're equal in this aspect, right? Then Hai looks better than Feng Ping."

Hong smiled, the skin around her nose crinkling slightly. "He doesn't look better to me."

"Ah, I forgot to show you something." Lilian clapped her hands and walked over to her desk. She pulled a drawer and took out a paper clipping as large as a palm. "Read this, and you'll think differently." She grinned.

Hong recognized that it was an article from *The Journal of Women's Health and Hygiene*. The title read "Don't Be Scared on Your Wedding Night." She lowered her head and read. In an elegant style the article described to the virgin reader the experience of losing her hymen on the first night. "It may hurt a little initially," the author wrote, "but do not panic. Ask him to be gentle. Gradually you will feel a pleasant sensation that you have not experienced before."

"Why do you want me to read this?" Hong's face reddened.

Lilian smiled. "Tell me what it's like."

"What?"

"The pleasant sensation."

"Damn you, how could I know!" Hong went for Lilian, waving her fist. Her almond eyes were shining and blinking.

"All right, I believe you, Little Nun." Lilian turned away. "God, I wish one of us knew." She sounded serious.

"Why did you say that?"

"Only by comparison can we tell who is better, right?"

"I don't get it."

"God, you're so naive. I wish lots of men were after me, and I'd do it with all of them. Too bad my parents didn't give me a pretty face like yours."

"That's silly."

"I mean it." Lilian kept her face straight. "If I were you, I'd do it with both of them and choose the better one."

"No, no, that's crazy. Once you sleep with a man, you'll never get rid of him. Don't you understand? Remember the girl who hanged herself because her ex-boyfriend talked about what they'd done? Nobody would marry me if I were known as 'a broken shoe.'"

"That's just an idea, but you should think of the physical part, shouldn't you?"

"How could I know?"

"See, that's why I said you should do it."

"No, I can't."

"At least you should think which one of them is abler, shouldn't you? I mean physically." Lilian rolled her eyes again.

"Damn you, Lilian. You have a dirty mind." Hong pinched her friend on the fleshy cheek.

"Come on, I said truth. Oh let go, let go!"

Hong released her grip. "To be honest," Lilian said, rubbing her cheek, "I think Pang Hai is better. He's taller and stronger."

"I don't know." Hong sighed.

It was already dark when Hong left Lilian's. A locomotive tooted its steam horn in the distance as the power lines were droning softly along the street. Hong thought of her friend's words and couldn't help smiling. Lilian had always been knowledgeable about things between a woman and a man, though she had never gotten good grades in school. "A muzzy head," as a math teacher had called her. Yet it was Lilian who, when they were in high school, had told Hong how babies were made. In her candid words, "Your dad did it to your mom, and then you were born." Before that enlightening moment, Hong had believed that if a woman sat together with a man in a dark movie theater she would be pregnant with his child.

Unlike Lilian, Hong had been disgusted with boys during her teens. In her eyes they were all rascals. When she was a sixth grader, she began to have her period. She was terrified at the sight of her blood and called out, "Mom, I'm bleeding!" Her mother, Mrs. Chen, smiled and said, "You're a big girl now." Then she found her a roll of soft gauze.

The next day in the PE class the students were running together around the playground. Suddenly Hong felt something passing through her trouser leg. She shuddered and almost fell down. She looked back and found the boys kicking forward her roll of bloody gauze and laughing and whooping. At this moment the recess bell rang. She hurried back to the classroom and buried her face in her arms on her desk, but the boys wouldn't let her off. Within half a minute a crowd gathered at the window shouting, "Bad girl," "Broken shoe," "Shameless," "Cracked melon." One of them was holding up a bamboo stick, on whose tip was exhibited that piece of scarlet evidence. Several small girls who hated her also joined them. Pang Hai and Feng Ping were among the crowd. Hong burst into sobs and dared not raise her head. Then the teacher ran over, grabbed the stick, and yelled, "Leave her alone, idiots!" She chased her students away, striking them so hard with the bamboo stick that it cracked.

That afternoon Hong drank a bottle of DDT at home; fortunately her mother found it out in time and took her to the Commune Clinic to have her stomach cleansed. At that time her father was the Party secretary of the commune, so the school leaders handled the incident very efficiently—the boy who had raised the stick was expelled.

It would be unfair to say that the boys always maltreated Hong. When the yellowish hair on their upper lips began to turn to soft mustaches in the high school, the chest of Hong's desk often received a chocolate bar, or an apple, or a pear, or a pomegranate, once even a baked sweet potato which was still warm. The donors always remained anonymous. Every time Hong handed the dainty to the teacher, who would take it home for her own children. The boys were brazen and despicable, and Hong was irritated by them, even believing that most of them were interested in her mainly because she had a powerful father. The more indifferent and elusive she was, the more charming and virtuous she grew in the boys' eyes. In her last year of high school she became the beauty queen, without winning any contest; the boys chose her in secret among themselves. Heavens, they would never leave her alone.

After her father died of bone cancer, life was hard for the Chens. Most of his former subordinates stopped showing any respect for his family. Two years after his death, the Chens were forced to move out of the compound inhabited by the cadres' families. Mrs. Chen begged some former friends to help, but nobody would intercede on her behalf. By now both the mother and the daughter had fully experienced the difficulty and humiliation caused by lacking power in their own hands. When several young men proposed to Hong, she told the matchmakers that she wasn't interested in marriage, but her mother persuaded her, saying, "If I die tomorrow, I won't be able to close my eyes unless you have a good husband." Every woman ought to marry; if she didn't, people would think her abnormal.

Because Hong didn't like any of the suitors, she began to focus her attention on their official positions. She remembered how prosperous and glorious the Chens had been when her father dominated Dismount Fort. The whole family had once taken a Russian jeep to Dalian City, the chauffeur obeying her father like a lapdog. She wanted people, especially those girls who hated and disparaged her, to look up to her again. Already the suitors without a presentable official position had retreated of their own accord; Feng Ping and Pang Hai emerged as the finalists. They knew Hong wanted to marry the vice-chairman-to-be, but neither of them could do anything to have himself elevated immediately, though they were both candidates for that position. All they could do now was force Hong to make her choice before the promotion materialized.

Feng Ping's matchmaker, Aunt Lin, visited the Chens two days later. She wanted them to give a definitive answer. Holding the tea Hong had poured her, the old woman turned to Mrs. Chen. "We can't wait anymore. You've got to let us know your decision in two or three days." She put the cup on the desk and shrugged her scraggy shoulders.

"Can't you give us another week?" Mrs. Chen said.

Aunt Lin sighed. "Only by agreeing to marry him before his promotion can Hong prove her love for Young Feng. He wants true love."

"Then tell him, go to hell," Hong said, her thin lips pursed.

"Shut up!" Mrs. Chen snapped at her daughter, and then turned to Aunt Lin. "She's totally spoiled. She doesn't mean it."

"Of course not. No girl's words mean business in her marriage. That's why we parents arrange things for them. But you've got to give us an answer soon."

At long last, the Chens agreed to make their decision in three days. Mrs. Chen was annoyed by her daughter's lack of preference. In such a foggy situation the only reliable chart was your own heart, but Hong couldn't feel anything. If pressed hard, she would say, "I don't want to marry, all right?" But she was wrong. She had to choose one or the other of the outstanding young men, whom most girls in Dismount Fort would kill to marry. In her heart Hong knew she must never lose such an opportunity. After this village there won't be the same inn, as the wise saying warns. But she felt sick at heart, wondering why people called a wedding "a Red Happy Event." What was it that you should be happy about?

Unable to choose, on the third day the mother and the daughter resorted to drawing lots. Mrs. Chen wrote "Feng" and "Pang" separately on two scraps of paper and rolled them into two tiny balls. She put them into a teacup. Covering the mouth of the cup with her palm, she shook it and dropped the paper balls on the glossy brick bed. "Now you pick one, Hong. Be careful, the one you choose will be your husband."

Hong shut her eyes and twisted the paper balls with her slim fingers, her face pale and her lips curled. "All right, I take this one." She handed it to her mother.

Mrs. Chen unrolled it. "No, you picked the wrong one!" On the paper the character "Pang" stood proudly.

"It doesn't matter," Hong said. "I'm going to marry him."

"Oh, my gut feeling is that Pang Hai is not going to be the chairman."

"It's too early to tell, Mom." Hong thought Lilian would be pleased by this choice.

On the same day the Chens' decision was known to most households in town. Pang Hai was elated. For him this was a good beginning. He felt his spine sturdier than before and even his heels seemed full of power when he walked. Of course he didn't know how the Chens had reached the decision. He had always kept an amorous eye on Hong since he came to know that she wasn't a bad girl at all and that the roll of bloody gauze only proved she was healthy and normal. As for the next step—the engagement, he hadn't lost his head over the initial victory and was inclined to make everything as simple as possible. At this critical juncture of his official career, he kept firmly in mind Chairman Mao's instruction: "We must always be modest and prudent and must, so to speak, tuck our tails between our legs."

He sent his matchmaker, Aunt Zheng, to the Chens to seek understanding: the engagement ceremony would be plain and quiet, whereas the wedding would be customary and colorful. The Chens didn't think it unreasonable, so it was settled.

The engagement dinner was held at the Pangs' on August 1, Army Day. Only a few guests were present. Besides the members of the two families, there were the secretary and the director of the Harvest Fertilizer Plant, where Pang Hai's father worked as a bulldozer driver. Aunt Zheng had also been invited, in addition to being presented a yard of woolen cloth by the

Pangs as "a little keepsake." The old woman wouldn't take money from such a good family and meant to do Hai a free service. Unfortunately she was sick on the engagement day, unable to come and eat.

At the dinner Hai couldn't help smiling at Hong, who would glare back. His eyes were so large they reminded her of an ox's. When he placed a chicken leg in her plate, the chopsticks slipped off his hand, which was huge and veined.

In the beginning the two tables were quiet, and the only words that could be heard were "Eat, try this," or "Fresh and crispy," or "Good fish, so fat." But after several rounds of sorghum liquor the men grew louder. The leaders of the fertilizer plant began talking of the housing program for their cadres and workers. Director Ma, a tall husky man, kept burping while drawing floor plans on the table with his fingers wet with alcohol. Liu, the stocky secretary, claimed he was so happy for the children that he must drink to his heart's content. Then he clapped his palm on his fat lips, remembering this was not the wedding. It didn't matter, however, because he would do that on October 1 when the young couple were scheduled to enter the bridechamber.

The older generation shook their heads again and again, sighing over how time was flying. It was as if yesterday when Hai and Hong had been small pupils in the Central Elementary School, but in the twinkling of an eye they became man and woman, ready to have their own children.

Mrs. Chen never liked the Pangs. Now and then she glanced at Mr. Pang and her son-in-law-to-be. They drank hard liquor with mugs and spat into an ashtray that sat right on the dining table. Mrs. Pang even sucked a mullet's head before their guests.

Hai's siblings, a younger brother and an elder sister, who had a baby girl and a husband working in Sand County, were drinking Gold Star beer with the noise of an exuberant creek. Meanwhile, Hong was sipping apple wine and her face was pink and shimmering, which made her resemble a young bride. She liked the sautéed tree ears, so her chopsticks kept transporting them into her small mouth.

"Ah," Director Ma cried and stood up. Before he could move a step he threw up—a yellowish shaft of liquid food splashed on the edge of the brick bed and the dirt floor. Immediately Mrs. Pang ran to the kitchen to get a bowl of vinegar to sober him up. Hong took a broom and a dustpan to remove the vomit. Hai's sister was helping too.

"Old Pang," Secretary Liu said, patting the bulldozer driver on the shoulder, "What a good daughter-in-law you have. See, she's begun to work. Hai is a lucky young man, to have such a nice girl." Then, giggling, he turned to Director Ma. "Old Ma, you're no good. One mug can throw you down like a corpse."

"Come, let's drink!" Ma's face was carmine, and he lifted Mrs. Chen's mug, which still had some soda in it.

Immediately Hai poured in some cold water. Ma clinked mugs with Liu and they drank up. "Good liquor," Ma said.

Then both mugs were refilled, though with different stuff, and together they emptied four mugs in a row.

Three minutes later Ma, filled with cold water, said he wanted to go out to pee. Liu stood up and said that he was going with Ma to the public latrine across the street, and that he didn't want to litter the outhouse in the Pangs' backyard. Obviously he was going to vomit. Hai held out a hand to support him. "Take care of your bride, young chairman," Liu said and stopped Hai's hand, "or you'll lose her. Ha ha—" He followed Ma out, staggering toward the front gate.

Mrs. Chen said Liu had no sense of propriety, and she reminded the others that he had once vomited on the county magistrate's leather shoes at a dinner. Mr. Pang, touching his right ear cropped by a piece of American shrapnel in the Korean War, agreed that the two leaders always liked to have a drop too many. Hong felt short of breath; the sour smell of the half-digested food scattered by Ma irritated her nostrils. She began to wonder how she could share the same roof with these savages. A sadness was rising in her chest. She wanted to weep. How she regretted having picked the paper ball. Why did she have to take a husband? She didn't need a man like Hai. Better to be an old maid than live with him and this family.

The more she thought about the engagement, the more heartbroken she became. Soon she was stuffing herself with the large pieces of chicken breast that had been put aside for the leaders. Then she pulled the platter of stewed mullet closer and munched one chunk after another, regardless of her mother's stepping on her foot and Mrs. Pang's squinting at her. She wanted to eat and eat and eat. If possible, she would have eaten up everything the Pangs owned. If they didn't like her, they had better break the engagement now.

Once in a while she glared at Hai, but to him her angry eyes were simply more charming, like blooming lilies. He was apparently tipsy and kept grinning at her boldly.

Then Director Ma burst in, gasping. "Come, help me stop Secretary Liu. He's walking in the street and shaking hands with everyone, even called a donkey 'my comrade.'"

Both Hai and his father lurched to their feet and rushed to the door, but before he could get out, Hai vomited on the threshold. His legs were shaky as he was running to the front gate, wiping his mouth on his sleeve.

"Swine!" Hong said under her breath. Her mother pinched her on the thigh under the table.

Aunt Zheng came to the Chens' twice the next week and asked for a list of gifts that the bride wanted from the Pangs. Because the wedding was scheduled for October 1, only seven weeks left, they should provide the list as soon as possible. Mrs. Chen said that she wasn't sure of what to ask for and must discuss it with Hong, who had been very busy recently, working a few extra evenings a week at the department store, doing a rush job of selling cotton cloth. The old matchmaker knew the Chens were waiting to see whether Hai would become the vice-chairman. If the promotion ended in his favor, they might want nothing, since nowadays power was more valuable than money and property.

The County Party Committee's decision on the promotion arrived at the Commune Administration the next Saturday. On hearing that Feng Ping was the lucky one, both Mrs. Chen and her daughter burst out crying. Hong wailed so loudly that even passersby on the front street could hear her. A number of children gathered at the window ledge and watched the big girl blowing her nose and wiping her tears and squirming on the brick bed. Her face seemed bloated with pain, her bangs stuck to her pale forehead. The children couldn't figure out what calamity had fallen on this household.

"She must've a stomachache, worms in her insides," said a boy.

"No, she lost her wristwatch."

"Why not report it to the police?"

In fact, Hong couldn't help missing another man, the only one she had ever liked. Three years ago, she had seen him playing volleyball against the Harvest Fertilizer Plant's team. She didn't know his name, though she heard that his team was from Tile County. While watching him play, she was longing to touch his square face and her heart was leaping. He wasn't handsome but looked so sweet and innocent. Afterwards she never tried to find out who he was, nor did she tell anybody how she felt. She thought herself silly and impractical, trying hard to forget him. For some reason, now all at once that young face came back to her, wrenching her heart.

Mrs. Chen came out and drove the children away. Though she couldn't stop her own tears, she didn't blame her daughter for not listening to her. Too late now. Damn the Pangs, she wished they had never existed.

Lilian came that evening. The two friends talked about the promotion. Although she understood how Hong felt—it must have been as if all your property was gone—Lilian still thought Pang Hai might be the better choice. This notion aroused Hong's interest. "Do you mean Pang Hai may have a good position in the future?" Hong said.

"No way." Lilian shook her head. "To tell you the truth, his official career may be over, because Feng Ping is above him now and can always step on him. He must hate Hai to the bones. A man can forgive everything except for murdering his father or stealing his wife."

"Then why did you say Hai was better?"

"Look at Feng, he's a monkey. At least Hai is like a man in appearance."

"For me they're the same. Hai is a gorilla." Hong smirked and rubbed her chest as though hit by her own words.

Now the list of gifts had grown. In addition to eight dresses, six satin quilts, a TV set, a Phoenix bicycle, a Shanghai wristwatch, and other expensive items, Hong insisted on a large banquet, fifty tables at least. She was not a girl who could be bought so cheap. Her mother felt uneasy about the banquet. "You know, dear," she said, "you shouldn't ask for such a thing, too costly. The wool comes from the sheep's own skin—you and Hai will be buried in debt."

"I don't care. If I can't live with him, I'll kill myself."

The Pangs agreed to every item on the list except for the banquet, not because they had to borrow the money (they might end up making a little profit, since by custom every guest would leave a good sum after he regaled himself), but because nowadays it was illegal to hold an extravagant wedding banquet. True, the peasants in the villages still squandered money away on food and liquor at weddings, but they were far away from the authority and could get away with it, whereas Pang Hai, a revolutionary cadre of the twenty-third rank, wouldn't take the risk.

But the bride was absolutely adamant, saying this was a once-in-a-lifetime event and had to be joyful and lavish. After Aunt Zheng traveled back and forth three more times, the Pangs finally yielded.

On the morning of October 1, National Day, Hong in a red flowered dress left home for the Pangs. She rode the new Phoenix bicycle and was accompanied by two bridesmaids, Lilian and Mingming, a salesgirl in the department store. On the backs of their bicycles they carried the bride's belongings, mainly clothes. The big pieces, like a cupboard and a pair of chests, had been shipped to the groom's house several days before. Mrs. Chen would come in an hour. The wedding was to take place in the Pangs' backyard, just a few blocks away.

It was a fine day. The sky was cloudless and a cool breeze was blowing gently. A few orioles were fluttering and twittering in the willows. On their way the bride and her maids were greeted by several cart drivers who whooped and cracked their long whips, and also by a group of little boys who made obscene gestures and chanted, "Slow down, my bride, you'll have a baby boy tomorrow night."

"That boy is your grandpa," Lilian shouted. Hong and Mingming kept pedaling quietly.

The banquet would start at two-thirty in the afternoon, because many guests came from villages over fifteen kilometers away; they would have to leave early, relinquishing the most delightful part of the wedding—busting the bridechamber, which would take place at night. The wedding ceremony was presided over by Secretary Liu, who wore a red paper flower in the buttonhole of his breast pocket, as though he were the bridegroom. He delivered a short speech, wishing the young couple longevity, a lifelong happy union, and a houseful of children and grandchildren.

Then together the bride and the groom sang two songs, "The East Is Red, the Sun Is Rising" and "Happy, We Must Not Forget the Communist Party." A few firecrackers exploded as candies and roasted peanuts were thrown in the air for the children, who rushed around and pushed each other like a flock of chickens pecking at grain. Some people wanted the couple to eat an apple, which would be held in the air by a thread so that the bride and the groom had to press their lips together to take a bite. But Director Ma told them, "Let's skip that part for the moment, and they'll do it after the feast." He also reminded them that there would be a lot of performance in the evening. The guests from distant villages were rather disappointed, but they were consoled by the fragrance of the dishes being cooked at the two brick ranges constructed specially for the wedding. They couldn't help turning their eyes to the four cooks in white hats. Two headless pigs, skinned and gutted, hung upside down beyond the kitchen shed.

Hong shuddered at the thought of chamber-busting. These boors could do anything, and she would be exhausted to death, having to control her temper and please these uncles and cousins. She remembered reading in a newspaper that at a village wedding three men had been killed by a chamber wall that had been busted as well and fallen on them. She told of her fear to Lilian, who assured her that she would keep her company at night and fight any man who dared to touch Hong.

Fried carps and whole chickens had been placed on the square tables. The first course, tenderloin sautéed with bamboo shoots, was being carried out in platters which resembled small barges. The guests were eager to see what wine and liquor they were going to drink. "See those large vats over there?" a young peasant said. "Screw his mother, I thought they had beer inside. Only vinegar and soy sauce were in them. Almost choked me just now."

Another man chuckled. "Serves you right. Who told you to steal a bowl of that?"

"They must've spent thousands for the feast, tut-tut-tut," an old man said. "Every part is so big."

Suddenly the back gate opened and the barrel of a rifle emerged, then a band of militia. "Don't move!" the tall commander ordered through a megaphone, his other hand raising a Mauser pistol. "This banquet is banned."

A whole company of militia rushed in, every man fully armed, even carrying four grenades and a filled canteen on the hips. Pang Hai went over to argue, but the commander ordered his guards, "Hold the groom in custody. Don't let him go." Then he announced to the stunned guests, "Now you are free to leave."

Nobody moved. Some of them had sent a gift to the Pangs or the Chens before the wedding, and many had saved their appetite for this feast by cutting both breakfast and lunch, so they all stayed. They saw a broad red flag flitting beyond the brick wall toward the back gate. Some children were singing the song "Destroy the Old and Set Up the New."

Before the song was finished, schoolchildren poured in. There were about three hundred of them and every one wore a red armband. The militia commander spoke through the megaphone again. "Comrades Small Red Guards, your task today is to wipe out the food. You must eat up this old feudal custom. Start now!"

Promptly the children split into fifty groups around the tables and began attacking the dishes. They didn't bother to pick up chopsticks, using their hands instead. Their cheeks swelled up as their jaws were crunching. Every bite they took was a sting in Pang Hai's heart. Suddenly Hai sprang away and rushed into the kitchen shed. Four militiamen followed him, shouting, "Halt, halt!"

Hai picked up a large shovel used for stir-frying and plunged toward a nearby table. He wanted to chop down a few of these little wolves. But before he could reach them, the militiamen seized him, pinned him to the ground, and removed the shovel. "I borrowed the money, I borrowed the money!" Hai groaned.

Women were crying inside and outside the house. Hong sat on the ground for a few minutes; then she got up and hid away in the haystack. Mr. Pang didn't lose his head and begged his leaders to intervene. Secretary Liu and Director Ma went up to the militia commander and talked with him. Five minutes later they returned, shaking their heads. "Feng Ping sent them here," Liu told Mr. Pang. Ma chimed in, "He's too high-handed." They dared not say more, because Feng was their superior now.

Meanwhile, realizing the banquet was gone altogether, the guests began leaving. However, some of them were so hungry they didn't leave without doing something. They smashed the soy-sauce and vinegar vats. Broken cups, plates, bowls were scattered everywhere in the yard.

"Feng Ping, I screw your ancestors one by one!" Hai yelled again and again, his mouth pointing to the sky.

Though cursing Feng Ping too, Lilian didn't lose her senses, and unlike Mingming, who had fled, she still remembered her duty as a bridesmaid. She had noticed Hong slipping to the haystack and tried keeping an eye on her. But when she went to fetch the bride half an hour later, Hong was no longer there! "Hong, where are you?" Lilian cried. Her voice reminded others of the delicate bride. No girl could stand such a blow. Mrs. Chen was mad, crying and plunging in vain at the militia commander. She wanted to take him to the Commune Administration to seek justice, but the man merely gave her a contemptuous look, his guards holding her back.

Meanwhile Hong was running toward the well on Old Folk Road. Tears were streaming out of her eyes, and she was too ashamed to face her mother and the in-laws now. It was she who had brought such a disaster on Hai and herself. The Pangs had spent four thousand yuan on the banquet alone and couldn't receive a fen in return. All the food was eaten up by the pupils. Oh, Hai and she would never be able to clear the debt. Such a miserable life was worse than death. Without thinking twice, she jumped into the dark well. To her surprise, it was not so deep as she had thought. The water barely reached her chest, but it was ice cold. She touched her thighs, her hips, her stomach, her breasts, her neck, and found every part of her body all right. She began trembling as she realized she had been merely a step away from the jaws of death. If she had plunged herself headlong, she would have killed herself easily by hitting the rocks. She groped around and felt the slippery wall covered with moss. It was impossible to climb out.

A moment later a metal bucket came down, hitting the rocky wall with a clank. Hong realized it was time to cook dinner and the well would be busy soon. She stuck her body to the wall and avoided standing in the way of the bucket, which floated on the surface of the water for a second, plunged in, came out full, and rose to the mouth of the well. Then another bucket descended and carried up a full load too. Hong raised her head to see who was up there, but she saw only the drawer's blue sleeves.

It occurred to her that this well was used by the people on three streets for drinking water. On Bath Street there was a well whose water had been sweeter than this one. Two years ago, the daughter of the Tangs on Blacksmith Road had drowned herself and her baby girl in that well because her husband and parents-in-law had scolded her for being unable to bear them a boy. People who had used the well for drinking water never stopped cursing the young woman. There were a lot of ways to kill herself, why did she choose this well? Because of the drowned bodies, no one would go there to fetch drinking water. Only a few families used the well for washing now. A pain seized Hong's heart. If she had died in here, she would have been a restless ghost, because everybody up there would have cursed her. Then she remembered her mother. How unfilial she was. When he was dying, her father had asked her to take good care of her mother, but she had forgotten everything and acted so foolishly. She burst into tears and blew her nose over the water. Another bucket was coming down. Hong held her breath.

Up on the ground a large-scale search for the bride was under way. Lilian had gone to Feng Ping's office and cursed him in front of his subordinates. At first Feng wanted to have her dragged out, but on hearing that she had told his mother on him—the old woman was waiting at home to scold him—and that Hong had disappeared, Feng restrained his temper and began to worry, sweat breaking out on his narrow forehead. Obviously the whole thing had gotten out of hand. If Hong killed herself he would feel guilty all his life. Such a nice girl, she shouldn't end up this way, in the hands of that rascal Pang Hai. With his squint eyes glittering, Feng told Lilian, "Stop blaming, all right? We must hurry and find Hong. It's terrible. I hope nothing will happen to her." Then he picked up the telephone and ordered the militia to search every dangerous cliff, ditch, pit, and hole in Dismount Fort and its vicinity, and report to him the minute they found her.

The militia in the Pangs' yard changed their attitude at once and joined the family looking for the bride. They went to the railroad station and the six bridges in town. They combed sev-

eral bushes and a few cornfields. Every reservoir in nearby villages was checked too. Nobody had seen a shadow of Hong, and
group by group the men returned empty-handed. Hai never
stopped cursing Feng Ping, declaring he would level the graves
of Feng's ancestors and annihilate the entire Feng clan if anything happened to his young wife.

It was almost dark. The half-moon cast a bluish curtain of
mist on the tiled roofs, the treetops, the streets. Light bulbs
flashed on one after another, and children were playing hide-
and-seek on the streets. The militia had gone home for dinner,
while the Pangs, Mrs. Chen, and Lilian were still searching. The
well keeping Hong had been looked and shouted into several
times, but Hong, clinging to the jagged wall, wouldn't respond
to the calling. She was uncertain who was up there and didn't
want to be surrounded by a crowd when she got out, though she
was trembling all over and her stomach was twinging with hunger and fear. Finally came a familiar voice. "Hong, are you down
there?"

"Yes, I'm here, Lilian!"

"My goodness, you are in there. Did you hurt yourself? Oh!"
Lilian broke into tears.

"No, I'm all right."

"Wait, we'll pull you out."

"Come back, Lilian. Come back." It was too late to stop Lilian,
who had left for help.

A few minutes later Hai and Mrs. Chen arrived with a rope
and a large bucket. Hai shouted into the well while sobbing and
lowering the bucket, "Hong, are you all right? Why do this to
yourself? It's not your fault . . ." Words just gushed out of his
throat. Never had he been so talkative.

Hong climbed into the bucket. "I'm in it now. Pull," she cried.

The second her feet touched the cement terrace, Hai embraced her and burst out wailing. "Even heaven collapsed, you shouldn't do this. How could I live without you!" Despite her dripping clothes, he held her tight as though afraid of losing her again. She felt his arms and chest so warm and so powerful that she let herself go, leaning against him as if nesting in a comfortable bed. Lilian was wiping her cheeks with a white handkerchief.

"My little devil, how could you abandon your old mother!" Mrs. Chen said while wrapping her daughter with a blanket. She was also unable to control her tears.

Hong was too overwhelmed to say a word. The street was shimmering in the moonlight. A smell of baked sweet potato was lingering in the air and aroused a pang in Hong's stomach. Together they walked back to the bridechamber, which would be safe and quiet for the first night.

■ Again, the Spring Breeze Blew

At her husband's funeral in the afternoon Lanlan cried so hard that she fainted and was unconscious for almost twenty minutes. The leaders of the production brigade assigned an oxcart to carry her back from the graveyard. Once home, she placed her one-year-old boy Kai on the brick bed and lay down beside him. Soon her sobbing subsided. She thought of returning to her mother's in Quarry Village the next morning.

She wasn't sure why she was so heartbroken. Certainly she missed her husband, but she couldn't tell whether she loved him so much as to cry her heart out for him. Since their marriage, they had fought almost every week. Now it was over. Two days ago, her husband had fallen from their house while repairing the roof. He broke his neck on the edge of a large water vat and died instantly without leaving her a word.

Outside, a hen began clucking. That's the black one, Lanlan told herself. Forty-six eggs now. Remember to boil ten for tomorrow's trip.

Eggs reminded her that her husband had died without food in his stomach. This again brought tears to her eyes. Though he had often beaten her, they had managed to live together; as the old saying attests: "One night's husband and wife guarantees a hundred days' affection." They had shared the same bed for twenty-two months and had been somewhat attached to each other. Besides, he had left her a son who was healthy and almost an exact copy of him.

Why am I so unlucky? she asked herself. I'm still young, just twenty-seven, a young widow. From now on, I'll have to take care of everything inside and outside the house, and have to be both mom and dad to Kai.

As if something tore at her heart, she sobbed again, mumbling to the pillows, "A young widow, a young widow."

It was getting dark. The smell of fresh corn cakes and fried soy paste began to fill Sea Nest Village. Sheep's bleating and pigs' squealing could be heard now and then. Lanlan didn't cook, but she knew she had to eat so as to nurse the baby. Lying in the dim room, she remembered Ailian, who had been a young widow for only a year and then married another man. But Ailian is a beauty in the village, she said to herself. I can't compare myself with her.

She heard a creak at the door. "Who is it?" she asked loudly. No sound. It must have been a dog, she thought. Since no food had been left in the outer room, she didn't bother to get up.

Suddenly the door curtain burst open and a man jumped in. "Keep quiet," he hissed, waving a long knife.

By instinct she turned to reach for the sleeping baby. "Don't move!" rasped the man.

She froze, staring at him. He was a small man, bony and pallid. His hair was long and unkempt, and his round eyes were glowing luridly. Though scared, she managed to ask, "What do you want?"

"I want your thighs." He grinned, revealing two broken teeth.

He moved close and ordered, "Take off your pants, and don't make any noise or I'll stab you and the little bastard." He pointed the knife at the baby.

A cramp stiffened her right leg, and she obeyed him, slowly untying her waistband.

"Quick, you bitch!" He stuck the knife into the waist of her pants and ripped it open. His left hand grasped a thick layer of flesh on her belly as his other hand stood the knife on the wooden edge of the bed. Then with both hands he pulled off her pants and briefs and threw them to the earth floor.

She was about to cry, but stopped at the sight of the knife. She was lying on the bed helplessly.

The man unbuckled his pants. "If you make a noise, I'll stab you through. Got it?"

She nodded, unable to say a word. He smelled of grass and mud; his belly was flat and hairy.

"Look at these thick thighs," he said, pinching her hip. "I thought I had luck today. Such an ugly thing. What lousy luck! These swollen udders." He fingered his long mustache. "Well, I guess I have to make do." He yanked at her breast and pressed his other hand on her shoulder.

With her nipple in his mouth, he began to enter her, moaning lustfully. Anger surged up in her. Slowly her hand moved to the knife, held it, pulled it off, raised it and thrust it into his rib cage. "Oh!" he gasped, and jumped up, tearing the cut open. The knife bounced off and hit the wall with a clang as her hand suddenly felt the warmth of his blood. He staggered away to the door. Then she heard a thump in the outer room.

Kai woke up with a cry. She grabbed the baby and dashed out, shrieking, "Help! Save my life! Help!"

In front of her, ducks and chickens were flapping and whirling. Two young cocks flew up and landed atop the latrine.

The villagers were bewildered by what had happened. Lanlan had run into the street screaming and wailing with the baby in her arms. She was wearing only a shirt, without anything on below her waist. Some men laughed and smacked their lips. Her neighbor Aunt Wang pulled her away to the Wangs' and gave her a pair of slacks. People went to Lanlan's house and found a half-naked man, pants around knees, in the outer room. His head was buried in the cornstalks beside the cooking range, while his bare butt pointed towards the ceiling. A few men kicked him, and he slid on his side, no breath left in him. A trail of blood led to the brick bed, on whose glossy surface was a crimson puddle. The big knife lying in a corner looked so expensive that a boy slipped it into his sleeve. The whole house smelled like a fish shop. Obviously, the man and the woman must have been doing it when he was struck down. Perhaps the spirit of the late husband had intervened.

How come on the very day of her husband's burial another man was found in her home? And both Lanlan and the man were half naked? Did they go to bed together? More confusing, nobody in the village knew the man. Who was he? Why did he choose to go to Lanlan's house and not another's? If he was a rapist as Lanlan claimed, how come he knew that no man was in her home today? What was their true relationship? Nobody could tell. It seemed there must have been something between them. This couldn't be a pure coincidence.

In the production brigade's office the Party secretary, Chian Heng, and the director, Zhang Gu, were restless. By Lanlan's appearance and account they were convinced that the dead man had attempted to rape her, though they were uncertain whether her denial of knowing him was true. During their questioning of her, she had never stopped crying and hadn't been able to describe everything clearly. More disturbing was that the man was killed, so whatever she said became the statement of one party. Nobody could prove the dead man was a rapist.

"Stop worrying about the evidence, Old Chian," Director Zhang said. "We'll never have it. The man is already dead. What really matters is who he is."

"That's true."

With a teacup in his hand the director went to a room across the corridor to call the police in Dismount Fort, while Secretary Chian remained in the office rolling a cigarette. In the next room Lanlan began crying again and declared she would kill herself for shame. A few female voices whispered, trying to calm her. Chian sighed and puffed out smoke. He had been a friend of Lanlan's late husband and knew the couple had gone through a tumultuous marriage, and he had never liked Lanlan since the day she came to the village.

Zhang returned, heaving a sigh. "Any news?" Chian asked.

"Only Shen Li is in town tonight. They'll come tomorrow morning."

"Does he know anything about the dead man?"

"He said there was a report on a missing man—Dong Cai's nephew, a lunatic."

Chian was shocked, because Dong was the vice-secretary of the commune. "Did he know what the madman looks like?"

"Yes, a small man in corduroy pants."

"Damn it," Chian slapped his thigh, "that's him."

"We're in trouble now."

Chian stood up and went to the next room. Zhang followed him. At the sight of them Lanlan winced and lowered her head. "You know who you killed?" Chian asked her. Without waiting for an answer, he added, "You killed Vice-Secretary Dong's nephew, a madman. Damn you, such a jinx."

Lanlan burst into tears again.

"Why did you say that?" asked Aunt Wang, who was Secretary Chian's mother-in-law's cousin. "What else could she do? Hothead Chian, what do you want your wife to do if a strange man is on top of her?"

"No matter what, she shouldn't kill him," Chian said. "Now he's dead, she can't prove her case and she'll go to jail." He shook his head.

"Let's go home. No use arguing with him," Aunt Wang said, and held Lanlan by the elbow. They stood up and moved to the door, followed by two other women.

After covering the corpse with rice straws in a storeroom inside the office house and assigning three militiamen to stand guard at the door for the night, the secretary and the director left for home. They assured each other that they had better stay off this mess and let the police handle it.

Lanlan and Kai stayed at the Wangs' that night. The fear and exhaustion upset her breasts, from which no milk came. She used to be proud of the two spurting fountains that had fattened the boy as if blowing up a balloon. Sometimes there had been so much milk in them that her husband had to suck them to relieve her pain, but now Kai, screaming, chewed her dry nipples ferociously with his two teeth. Aunt Wang gave her a large bowl of rice porridge; Lanlan fed the boy with it and ate two sweet potatoes herself.

Kai fell asleep soon afterwards, but Lanlan couldn't stop tossing and turning in bed. She worried about what was going to happen the next day. Are they going to send me to jail? she asked herself. For sure they will. I killed an important man. Tears streamed down her cheeks again. What should I do about Kai if I go to jail? Oh, I'm such an unfortunate woman. Today I buried my husband and tomorrow I'll squat in a dark cell. Whose fault is this? I was defending myself and that man was going to kill me, but they won't believe me. Oh, what a life, so miserable, one misfortune after another.

It serves you right, she cursed herself. The moment your husband was buried, you began thinking how soon you would get married again, thinking of another man. It serves you right. Now you have a man and you can't get rid of him. Shameless, you can't live without a man.

The self-scathing words seemed to make her feel a little better. With her stomach gurgling from time to time, she wept continually until she fell asleep.

Early next morning Aunt Wang accompanied Lanlan back to her house. On the ground, in the outer room, there were a few large patches of dried blood. With a coal shovel Aunt Wang scraped them off; she brought in some fresh earth with a basket and covered the spots with it. They stamped about to tamp down the earth. Then they used water and towels to wipe off the blood on the bed. Because the bed's surface was made of oilpaper, it wasn't hard for them to get rid of the blotches and stains. After the cleaning Aunt Wang left. Still, the house smelled fishy, so Lanlan opened all the windows.

Having tied one end of a rope to the window frame and the other end around Kai's waist to prevent him from falling off the bed, Lanlan began to bake corn cakes and make glue. She kept telling herself she had to eat—it would be a long day. Oddly enough, though she knew she might be sentenced to prison, somehow in her heart she felt the whole thing wouldn't turn out that ugly. Hard as she tried to take the matter seriously, she seemed quite certain they would let her return home in the evening. She went out to feed the chickens, ducks, and piglets. At the sight of the food—chopped radish greens mixed with corn flour—the poultry made so much noise that Widower Bao, Aunt Wang's brother-in-law, who happened to be passing by, stopped at the front gate to watch and whistle. Lanlan dared not raise her eyes to look at the man, who had a wry mouth.

The moment she put down her bowl on the dining table, two young men came to take her to the brigade's office. They said that the police would arrive at any time and that she must go with them without delay. She left Kai with Aunt Wang and went with the men. Unable to keep herself from imagining the inter-rogation, she began to retch and had to stop at the roadside. She sat down on her haunches and vomited several minutes. Stand-ing up, walking another few steps, she had a cramp in her right leg again. The two militiamen had to pull her along like drag-ging a counterrevolutionary to a public denunciation. She was moaning all the way.

When they reached the entrance to the office two policemen were already in there. A stalwart middle-aged man—the director of town police, Zu Ming—came out to meet her. Surprisingly, he smiled at her and held out his large hand. "Congratulations," he said in a clear voice.

Lanlan was bewildered and dared not stretch out her hand. All the brigade leaders were standing behind the policemen and smiling at her without any trace of ill feeling. She was gawking at them.

"Congratulations, Comrade Lanlan," Zu said again, coming closer. She gave him her hand. He shook it and said, "We heard from the County Police this morning that a prison escapee had entered our area. He raped a woman in Sand County two days ago. The man you killed yesterday is the very criminal on the loose. Thank you, comrade. You helped us get rid of a class enemy. You must've had a terrible fright. Please forgive us for coming so late."

Without a word, Lanlan collapsed to the ground. She cried at the brigade leaders, "I told you it's not my fault, but you didn't believe me." She gasped for breath, kicking her feet and wiping her eyes with the back of her hand. "Everybody blamed me for his death. You all bully me, a poor woman who just lost her husband. Oh where, where can I find justice!"

With a red face Secretary Chian went up to her and said, "Lanlan, don't be so upset. It's over now. The man isn't the lunatic, and we made a mistake. You did a good thing. We're all proud of you."

Director Zhang meanwhile told a young man to bring over a strong bicycle, a Big Golden Deer, to carry her home.

Though the case was resolved, Lanlan didn't seem to feel better. In one week two men had died in her house. What else could she be but a jinx to men? Who would dare to come close to her? She knew that the villagers thought her this way and that she would have to remain a widow for a long time. Looking in a mirror, she found herself resembling her aged mother more than before: her round eyes had grown broader, two dark curves appeared beneath the lower eyelids, her mouth was sunken a little, her lips took the shape of a heart, only her nose was still delicate and pretty. A gray hair stuck out on her forehead; she got hold of it and pulled it off. It was a long one and she threw it to the ground. She remembered the saying: "One smile makes you look ten years younger, while one worry turns your hair white."

That evening Aunt Wang came. She sat on the edge of the brick bed and put Kai on her lap. The boy gave out laughter as the old woman stuck her head again and again in his belly, tickling him. Lanlan poured a cup of boiled water for Aunt Wang and sat down at the other end of the bed.

Then the old woman said what was on her mind; she wanted Lanlan to consider marrying Widower Bao.

Though Aunt Wang said they were a natural couple, Lanlan couldn't help knitting her brows. That man is almost fifty, she thought. He's too old for me. She's making fun of me. He could be my father.

Aunt Wang seemed to read her thoughts and said, "Lanlan, don't think he's old. Look at the way he walks, and the strength he shows when working in the fields, and his big hands and thick shoulders. Don't tell me that man is old. Oh, my goodness, what an appetite he has. He eats a basin of noodles at one—" She held her tongue and regretted mentioning his appetite, since no woman liked a big eater. She added, "An older man is more considerate, you know."

"Aunt Wang, I'll think about it," Lanlan said.

"All right, take your time. We'll wait for your answer."

After the old woman left, Lanlan felt tired and decided not to go to her mother's so soon. She would stay home for a few days to recover from the exhaustion.

The next evening Aunt Wang came again. From then on she came almost every day, playing with Kai and helping Lanlan with housework. Lanlan didn't like it, and by and by she was annoyed by the old woman's presence in the house. For sure she was grateful to her, for sure she would do something in return, but not marrying her brother-in-law in such a hurry. Of course, she knew that since the villagers thought of her as a jinx, there would be few men who were interested in her, but why couldn't she wait? She was not so cheap that she would make do with any man, even an old scarecrow like Widower Bao. She was not so weak that she couldn't live without a man in her house. Some-day she might marry a man who was even better than her late husband. Things would change as long as she waited patiently. Who knows, the spring breeze may blow again, she kept saying to herself.

A week later a middle-aged reporter arrived at Sea Nest Village. His task was to write about Lanlan's brave deed. At the interview in her house, he had her describing the event from the begin-ning to the end. The brigade leaders accompanied the reporter, and Secretary Chian kept saying she was the best young wife in the village.

Lanlan couldn't understand why there was so much glory in killing a man, vicious as that thug was. She wouldn't do it again. No, even for ten thousand yuan she wouldn't. So she told them plainly, "I was scared. I am still scared. I've burned all the clothes

I wore that day. At night I always see a shadow in the outer room. Sometimes I wake up screaming like a man's on top of me. Oh heaven, I can still smell him in the house."

The reporter smiled amiably and said, "Don't be so scared. You'll get over it soon." He was writing down her words.

She noticed that his hands had long fingers. The black fountain pen was moving rapidly and spitting out one character after another. She had never seen such male hands, which apparently had nothing to do with farm work. None of the women in the village had hands so delicate. She gazed at his handwriting, which was beautiful. He must be a good writer, who could make words flow like a stream and float like clouds.

When she added water to their teacups, she stole a glance at the reporter. He was handsome, with a pale face, a mouth having upward corners, and a straight nose. His large eyes had double-fold lids. In every way he was different from those country men she knew. She found herself breathing strangely and couldn't help glancing at him time and again.

The interview ended, and the men stood up and were ready to leave. Lanlan asked them to stay for lunch, saying she would cook long noodles with oysters, but Director Zhang said the brigade's kitchen had prepared a meal. She realized they would have a feast there, so she didn't insist.

They went out of the house. The reporter thanked her and shook hands with her. His hand was smooth and warm. She watched them walking to the front gate. He was taller than the other men and his gait was full of ease.

"Lanlan, you're in the newspaper," Ailian shouted when they were hoeing beets four days later.

"Really? What does it say about me?"

Ailian read the article in *Red Star,* the county's newspaper, to Lanlan and the villagers gathering around. The title said, "A Brave Woman and Good Wife." The article described how Lanlan had fought an escaped criminal to protect her chastity; she was so brave and so determined that she wrestled with the man and stabbed him to death. It ended with a petition that such a good woman deserved a reward, just as a soldier would be awarded a merit citation or a promotion for his outstanding service.

All the commune members in the field congratulated Lanlan, but she was puzzled a little. She wasn't that good. When she stabbed the thug she had never thought of her husband at all, not to mention preserving her chastity for him, a dead man. But she didn't say anything, because she believed the handsome reporter must have helped her in secret. She mustn't appear as if she didn't know how to appreciate favors. Calm though she seemed, she couldn't concentrate on the hoeing. Again and again her hoe cut down some seedlings. She cursed herself under her breath and kicked tufts of weeds to cover up the felled beets.

From that day on, all the brigade leaders became very considerate to her. They asked her whether she wanted help for sowing her family plot and whether her piglets needed gelding. Whatever she was unable to do, just let them know. In a week another article appeared, but this time in the biggest newspaper in the province, *Liaoning Daily.* It praised Lanlan as a model in fighting class enemies, as the title declared: "A Young Woman Subdued a Violent Criminal." Currently, the Provincial Administration was waging a full-scale campaign against crime. The article called upon all citizens to follow Lanlan's example and participate in cracking down on the criminals so as to create a peaceful environment for everyone to work, study, and live in.

Now Lanlan became famous. The County Administration issued a document about her case, instructing the Personnel Department to assign her a good job and the Police Bureau to provide her with a residence card, which would qualify her as a city dweller. In a few days she was informed that she was given a job as a saleswoman at a hardware store in Gold County. She would be paid sixty yuan a month, 30 percent higher than the regular starting salary. In addition, she would become a permanent resident in the county town.

No one expected such a fortune could drop from heaven. Aunt Wang was unhappy about it, because Lanlan hadn't given her an answer yet and probably had stopped considering the proposal. Now the young widow had flown beyond the old woman's reach, and Widower Bao's chance of marrying her was dwindling. One morning Lanlan heard beyond the wall Aunt Wang cursing a dog, "You ungrateful beast." Lanlan didn't care. Her mother had arrived to help her after hearing of what had happened, and her breasts had regained abundant milk, and she didn't need to have anything to do with that jealous crone anymore. At last Aunt Wang showed her true nature. A yellow weasel never wishes a chicken a Happy New Year without thinking of the chicken's blood, Lanlan told herself.

Two weeks later *The People's Daily,* the largest newspaper in China, also published a short article about Lanlan. In addition to praising her virtue and bravery, it mentioned her residence card and her new job, which she actually couldn't start in two months until an old clerk retired from the hardware store. This article brought her hundreds of admiring letters from different parts of the country. Dozens of men sent her letters containing their photographs and proposed to her. Most of them were soldiers in the army or farmers in the countryside. They didn't care what she looked like, because they knew she was good—a chaste, healthy woman; and they wanted nothing but a virtuous, hardworking wife. Some men even said they would treat the baby boy as their own.

Lanlan was stunned that all of a sudden so many men would marry her, ready to give her a happy family. For the first time in her life she felt China was indeed a great country and never lacked men and women. But her mother was coolheaded and told her that besides their interest in her virtue and health, most of the men also had an eye on her residence card and her lucrative job. They wanted their descendants to be city dwellers, since according to the law an infant automatically adopted its mother's residential status. She told Lanlan, "Men are always after a good woman, just like flies after blood." So she helped her choose a reliable man, who was from their home village and worked as a cook at a state-owned restaurant in Gold County. The wedding was scheduled to take place at the Mid-Fall Festival. By then, Lanlan would have settled in the county town.

Sometimes she couldn't help thinking of the handsome reporter. She regretted that she hadn't asked his name. The memory often brought up a slight contraction in her chest, but she tried not to let it disturb her mind. In secret, she regarded him as a benefactor, an upright gentleman, and probably a sage. Now the spring breeze did blow, and she got more than she had expected. You mustn't be too greedy, she kept telling herself. Besides, that man must have had his own family and never have thought of her—a simple rustic woman. Whoever he was, she wished him lots of children and a happy life.

■ Resurrection

"Damn you," Fulan cursed her husband, Lu Han. "Now the whole Ox Village knows you slept with my sister. How can I go out and meet their faces?"

Lu was sucking at a pipe in silence. The wrinkles on his forehead stretched to his temples, and his small eyes were lusterless. He was not yet thirty, but he had changed so much recently that he looked like a man in his fifties. Fulan took their four-month-old boy off her large breast, turned him around, and thrust her other nipple into his mouth. She said, "Shame on you. Can't take care of your own cock. Even a studhorse knows not to mount his sister. Shameless—why don't you go out, find a tree, and hang yourself?"

Lu wanted to jump up and yell, "Your sister's no good either, a cracked melon already! If a bitch doesn't raise her tail, no dog can do anything to her." But he remained on the bench, motionless, biting his thick lips.

"All right," she started again, "play deaf if you like. Tomorrow I'll go back to my parents with Leopard. If your face is thick enough, come and fetch us. My dad and brothers will skin you alive."

Lu stood up and walked out into the dusk. He knew that talking was useless; once she got an idea into her head, you could never bring her around. Besides, what could he say? He was in the wrong to have slept with Fuli when his wife was pregnant. He felt so ashamed that he had cursed himself many times, but what was done was done, and all he could do now was bear the consequences.

The peanut plants rustled in a lazy breeze. Katydids were chirping tremulously as the night air brought its coolness. Lu sat down by a millstone under a large mulberry. His broad shoulders drooped, and his short legs wearied. He gave out a long sigh and muttered to himself, "You asked for it."

He began thinking about how to atone for his error and start his life anew. The day before, the Party secretary, Zhao Mingyi, had told him to prepare to make a clean breast of his offense. He was supposed to go to the production brigade's office the next evening and face interrogation by the brigade leaders. He was not afraid of their scolding, because he was certain he could keep quiet and endure their scathing words. What worried him was that if they were not satisfied with his confession and self-criticism, they could have him denounced publicly or paraded through the streets as a corrupt element. If that happened, his family and he himself would be done for. He had to be careful not to offend those leaders. For the time being, he thought, let Fulan do whatever she wants. He should deal with the external crisis first. Only after settling that could he put his family in order again.

Next morning, after breakfast, Fulan was ready to leave with their baby for Date Village, where her parents lived. She was to take a horse cart, which was going there to carry back peanut cakes for the brigade's chicken farm. Before she got on the cart, Lu gave the driver, Chu, a packet of Rose cigarettes and asked him to take care of his wife and son on the way. Chu smelled the cigarettes and promised with a grin, "They'll get there without losing a hair."

After they left, Lu went directly to the soybean field on the southern hill and joined the commune members in hoeing.

He didn't cook lunch for himself at noon; instead he ate two cold corn cakes and radishes with soy paste. After feeding the poultry and the sow and the piglets, he went back to the field. For a whole day he smoked continually, musing over the impending trial. How lucky it was that his parents were dead. If they had been alive, the shame he brought on them could have killed them. How lucky he was that the leaders hadn't caught Fuli, or they would have interrogated her to see whether everything he told them was true. She had left for her aunt's in Heilongjiang Province a month before the scandal became public. In the northern frontier every woman was considered marriageable, because men outnumbered women. Two brothers would even share one wife. Lu heard that Fuli became engaged to a middle-aged veteran soon after she arrived there.

At seven in the evening Lu reached the brigade's office. The door was open, and inside the room the radio was playing a song, "I See the Pole Star When I Look Up." Lu stepped in, but dared not go farther; he stood by the door waiting for instructions. Secretary Zhao, the brigade director Wang Peng, and Scribe Hsiao sat at a table smoking cigarettes and drinking tea. Zhao motioned to Lu to sit in front of them. The scribe turned off the radio. The room grew quiet, but Lu could hear a droning sound made by a few flies. He was reminded of the lines from a poem by Chairman

Mao: "On our small planet / A few flies bang on walls / Buzzing, moaning, sobbing."

The trial started. Zhao pointed at the scroll hung on a wall beneath the Chairman's portrait, and ordered: "Read these words for us."

"Leniency Toward Those Who Confess; Severity to Those Who Refuse!" Lu read in a shaky voice.

"Good," Zhao resumed, "you understand the Party's policy, so I won't waste my breath explaining it to you. Your attitude towards your crime will determine how we handle your case."

Lu was struck by the word "crime." Is adultery a crime? he asked himself. It must be. Then they can treat me as a criminal, a class enemy! Sweat broke out on his forehead. The thought occurred to him that he ought to appear more remorseful.

"Tell us, when did you start the abnormal relationship with Lin Fuli?" Wang asked.

"Last fall," Lu said.

Scribe Hsiao dipped a pen into an inkstand and started taking notes.

"How many times did you two have sexual intercourse?"

"I can't tell exactly."

"Think hard." Wang's eyes drilled into Lu's face and made him shudder a little. "Tell me, how many times?"

"Probably twenty."

"How many times did you go to bed together?"

"Mmm—once."

"Why only once?"

"Because my wife was home all the time. She went to town to sell chickens that day, so we two slept together on the warm bed."

"What day was that?"

"I can't remember exactly. It was last winter."

"Your wife was carrying your baby at that time?"

"Yes."

"Shame on you!" Wang thumped the table. "Your woman was big with your child and went to town selling chickens for you, while you were screwing her sister at home. What kind of a man do you think you are?"

"I'm sorry." Lu hung his head low.

"Sorry, too late," Wang shouted. Then he moved his head closer to Lu and asked in a soft voice, "Why did you do that?"

"I don't know. Couldn't contain myself."

"No, it's not a problem of self-control," Secretary Zhao broke in. "You have too many bourgeois thoughts in your brain. Though you're a descendant of a poor peasant, those thoughts have corrupted your mind and driven you to commit the crime."

"Yes, that's true," Lu admitted.

"Tell us why you had sex with both your wife and her sister," Wang resumed. "What's the difference between them? Aren't they dishes from the same pot?" Wang's baggy eyes searched Lu's face.

"Don't know. I can't tell the difference." Lu was bewildered by the question, but he told the truth. He had never thought of differences between the two women.

"All right, let's come back to the first time. Where did it happen?" Wang asked.

"In the sorghum field by the reservoir."

"Talk more about it. Describe how you two met there, who started it, what you said to each other, how you did everything there. From the beginning to the end."

"I've forgotten the details."

"Lu Han . . ." Secretary Zhao spoke in a serious voice. "You've been trying to evade the questions. I hope you understand that this attitude will put you in an awkward situation, which will require us to take necessary measures."

"Yes, I do, I do."

"Tell us everything then," Wang went on. "Who can believe you forgot the first time."

Lu began weeping. "I don't remember clearly."

"All right, tell me who opened pants first?"

"Mmm—, she o-opened mine."

"See, you remember it well. Then what did she do?"

"She, she—"

"Don't mince your words."

"She took me into her mouth."

The secretary, the director, and the scribe all chuckled but immediately became solemn again. Lu kept his head low and dared not look at them.

"What did she say?" Wang asked.

"I can't recall."

"We're sure you remember. You refuse to tell us, don't you?"

"No, I don't."

"Tell us then."

"She said, said—"

"Said what?"

"She said, 'I love this—this chunk of flesh best.'"

They burst out laughing. Lu shuddered, his face covered with sweat. A cold tingle ran down his spine. He knew he had said too much. The villagers would soon know what he said, and other villages would hear of those words as well; his in-laws, too humiliated, would chop him to pieces.

"Tell us, did your wife ever do that to you?" Wang asked.

"No." Lu shook his head.

"See, that's the difference. Just now I asked you why you ate two dishes from the same pot. You said you don't know. You're dishonest, lying to us. How can you receive any clemency?"

Lu wiped the tears and sweat off his face. He hated himself for having incurred such a misfortune—his family was broken and he could easily become a reactionary element. Everything had happened because he hadn't been able to control his penis and had never thought of the consequence. Why couldn't he wait for his wife until she gave birth to the child? His woman was much prettier than her sister. It served him right. However hungry, he shouldn't have taken food indiscriminately.

Secretary Zhao whispered in Wang's ear. They apparently had to go somewhere for a meeting or a party. Wang nodded, then turned to Lu. "We stop here for today. This is just a beginning, and you haven't shown us a sincere attitude yet. Go home and write out your confession. Describe every meeting with her to the smallest detail. Don't leave out anything on purpose. We can tell where you play a shoddy trick. Is that clear?"

Lu looked at Wang and then at Zhao. His face contracted nervously and produced a false smile.

"We know you can write," Secretary Zhao said. "You're one of the few middle-school graduates in our Ox Village. If you can't write, nobody can."

"Yes, that's why you always carry that thing," Wang said, pointing at the Gold Dragon fountain pen stuck in Lu's breast pocket. Then he turned to the scribe and ordered, "Young Hsiao, give him stationery."

Hsiao came over and put before Lu five pads of letter paper, two bottles of blue ink, three brand-new penholders, and a small box of nibs. "All are yours," Hsiao said.

Lu took the stationery, stood up, and made a bow. He put on his cap and turned to the door.

For two days Lu worked on the first page of his confession. Indeed, he had written well in middle school and even won a prize for an essay on the advantages of planting trees, but he had never tried this sort of writing. In addition, he was uncertain what he should put into the confession. Whatever he wrote on paper would be kept in his file and could be used against him in the future. Moreover, those leaders would surely pass the writing around, and the whole village would read it. Some people had already known what he said two days before. This morning, while he was cutting grass for the geese near the village entrance, Chu drove the horse cart by, cracking his long whip and chanting, "I like this chunk of flesh best! I like this chunk of flesh best!" How he hated Chu. How he wanted to grab that whip, flog him to the ground, and thrash all the breath out of him. He regretted giving Chu a packet of cigarettes worth twenty-three fen.

No, he must not say anything like that again. It was a matter of life and death. He envisaged his four brothers-in-law, led by their father, brandishing scythes and spades in search of him. Even the two screaming sisters-in-law wanted to scratch and bite him. From now on, every word he said had to be carefully thought out.

On the other hand, if he didn't satisfy the leaders, they could handle his case in whatever way they liked. They could punish him as a criminal, to warn those who dared to disobey them. Or, at least, they could assign him an extra amount of work every day in the name of reforming him through labor. However well he wrote, he could never please both his in-laws and the leaders.

Full of remorse, he again cursed himself and regretted having the affair with Fuli. Life was so miserable. He had done himself in without second thoughts. If only he could have stopped lusting for women. How wise were Buddha's words: Desire and lust were the source of disaster. He looked down at his crotch and cursed his penis again. The little devil always went its own way.

He was supposed to turn in the confession the next evening, but he was still on the first page. He had quoted a long passage from Chairman Mao, criticized himself with severe words, and talked about the liberal nature of his offense. Yet these items formed only a beginning to the confession. He had to fill out several pages at least. He was beating his brains about how to continue.

Having mused for hours, he decided to write about the day when they went to bed together. He began with how he had seen his wife off with the chickens in front of the tofu plant, and how he had carried back two buckets of water from the eastern well. When he returned, Fuli was naked on the large brick bed waiting for him. She asked him to bolt the front door, which he did. At first he felt uneasy; then he let himself go and did it with her.

He managed to draft three pages and copied them out in clean handwriting. After reading the manuscript aloud twice, he felt pretty good about it.

The next evening he took the confession to the brigade's office in hope of persuading the leaders of his sincerity. The same men waited for him. Unlike the last time, a mug of hot tea was on the desk before Lu.

After glancing through the confession, Secretary Zhao handed it to the scribe and asked him to read it out, since Director Wang was illiterate. Zhao lit a cigarette and blew the smoke toward Lu, his narrow eyes fixed on Lu's sallow face. Lu trembled and looked away.

No sooner had Hsiao finished reading than Wang stood up and pointed at Lu's nose. "What goddamn confession is this? Screw your ancestors. Three pages full of farts! You took away five pads of good paper but returned only three pages of rubbish. Do you want to confess or not?"

"Yes, I do. S-sorry, I'm still learning how—how to write."

"Your confession does include one truthful sentence, though," Secretary Zhao put in. "Do you know what one?"

"No, I don't. Please enlighten me."

Zhao picked up a page and read it out. "When I was back with the water, I saw her lying on the bed stark naked, like a huge fresh ginseng-root." He threw the page on the desk and asked, "Do you know why I say it's a good sentence?"

"No, I don't."

"Because it tells what you saw and how you felt at that very moment."

"Yes," Wang said, "Secretary Zhao's right. Write like he said. Don't cut corners."

"We give you a week for a complete confession," Zhao said deliberately.

"Go home," Wang ordered, "and recall all the twenty times.

Write down all the facts and details. Make no less than a hundred pages."

Lu managed to get up, but forgot to bow before moving to the door. With his head heavy and something like mosquitoes buzzing in his ears, he staggered out of the office.

He slept only three or four hours every night, working hard on the confession. Still, he wrote no more than five pages and was uncertain if they were acceptable. Of course he dared not tell them anything in detail. That would destroy his sister-in-law's life. The leaders would surely send a letter to the local Party branch in charge of the area where Fuli was now. Who would want to marry her if everybody knew of what they had done in the cornfields, in haystacks, in bushes, in pigpens, in the pump house? A detailed confession would also ruin his own family— his wife would never come back with his son. He was very lucky that his first-born was a boy, because the rule allowed nobody to have a second child. His luck was what made others jealous, particularly Director Wang, who had only a granddaughter. Because he was a leader and a Party member, Wang couldn't allow his son's wife to have another child, thus breaking the rule that everyone was eager to tamper with. Those bastards—they could never bear to see others' happiness.

Lu's eyes grew bleary from writing under an oil lamp. Though full of self-disgust, he constantly imagined different ways to get out of the trouble. He knew he could never meet the standard set by the leaders. More than a hundred pages? That was a book, and they might make many copies of it. The whole village would read it, and probably all the commune cadres too. He was no writer and had no time to learn to be one. Even if he were, he wouldn't dare to write such a book. But in two days he would have to hand it in; by no means could he get it ready. How, oh how could he find a way out of the crisis?

He thought of giving gifts to the leaders, but he wouldn't have any real money until the end of the year, when the brigade's annual account was settled. Those leaders wouldn't accept promises. Four months remained—and no distant water could quench the fire here and now. However, one thing continually came to his mind and tickled his brain: General Chou's Shrine at Sea-Watch Cliff was said to be about to open after being in ruins for eight years. The temple had been built in memory of a national hero, Chou Wu, who a hundred years ago led the Chinese troops and civilians in burning the ships of the Japanese invaders and driving them back into the sea. In order to inspire patriotism among the Chinese, the present government decided to restore it. Lu heard that the temple was under repair and that monks were being recruited.

The ocean of misery has no bound, he thought; repent and the shore is at hand. Why don't you give it a try? Good, quit the whole thing. I'll leave this mess behind and go into the mountain. For sure, they won't bust the temple and drag me out. That would violate the Party's religious policy and they would get themselves into trouble. Being a monk, I'll have time to study, have food and clothes always, and no worry about earthly affairs. I'm fed up with the farm work here. You work your ass off but get no pay if the harvest is poor. Fulan has her place to go; I too have somewhere to stay. I won't come back, even if she begs me on her knees. Let her learn a lesson from being a widow with a husband alive.

What if you don't like the temple? Why worry so much? If

it's no good in there, you can always come back. Who'll force you to be a monk? No time to waste; you must leave as soon as possible. Hide away for a while. In a few weeks I'm sure they'll lose interest in the case. At least I'll have enough time there to figure out a new way to deal with them.

A few lines of Chairman Mao's poetry echoed in his mind: "Many things must be done in a hurry / Heaven and earth spin— time presses / Ten thousand years are too long / We must seize every hour." Yes, go. The longer the night lasts, the more night- mares will come up.

He got up, grabbed his pen, and wrote on a blank sheet of paper,

Respectable Leaders:

Having understood the gross nature of my crime, I have decided to become a monk. I love our country and am grateful to the Party, but I feel too ashamed to face anybody in the village, so I am leaving now for a temple where I can continue self-examination and self-education. I will study hard there and live a new, peaceful life. Farewell, my dear comrades.

Yours guilty,

Lu Han

P.S. Please inform my wife of my leaving so that she can come back and take care of the house and the pigs. I really appreciate this.

He wrapped into a blanket his summer clothes and his only two packets of Great Gate cigarettes, and tied them up with a rope. With all his secret personal savings—eleven yuan—in his pocket, and the clothes bundle on his back, he went into the kitchen and drank two scoops of cold water. He returned to blow out the lamp, then walked into the dark.

The night was cool and moonlit, filled with insects' chirring and frogs' croaking. He was not afraid of wolves. What he really feared was man, to him the most vicious animal and the most dangerous thing, because only man knew how to trap you. He ran as fast as he could and forced himself not to listen to any distinct sound. Fortunately, the temple was not far away, only four and a half kilometers from Ox Village. In twenty minutes it emerged in the distance. The glazed tiles shimmered in the moonshine, and the curved eaves stretched along the ridge of a hill and were shaded by the huge crowns of trees. On the roof perched the statuary lions and tigers that seemed alive and ready to stand up and patrol like guarding gods. What a view, Lu thought; it must be a place where immortals visit. He hastened his steps and felt he had made a wise decision. Anyone who lived in that majestic temple would enjoy longevity and happiness. Yes, he said to himself, go there, and forget the hubbub and turmoil at home.

At once his body became light, as if he were flapping a pair of wings through the air. Within half an hour he stood at the front entrance of the temple, striking the wooden gate and shouting, "Open the door!"

After a short while a noise came from inside. He heard someone coughing and shuffling to the entrance. Beyond the high stone wall flickered the light of an oil lamp. "Who's there?" an old man's voice asked.

"Master," Lu said, feeling his heart in his throat, "I came to study gods with you. Please open the door and let me in."

"What do you really want in the middle of the night?"

"To be your disciple. Please open the door."

With a screech a hole six inches square was revealed on the gate, and a column of light thrust out. Lu moved closer and saw the old monk's chubby face, gray hair, smiling eyes. He had a large wart beside his crimson nose.

"Master, I want to be your student."

"Young man," the monk said, "I do want to take a lot of students, but so far I don't have any. I've no say in this."

"Take me please, Master. I can read and write. I can work and cook."

"Like I said, I want to, but I have no say in hiring."

"Hiring? You mean I have to be hired?"

"Yes, employed. Everybody wants to be a monk all of a sudden. It's like seeking employment. No, more than a job, it's like going to college. A new monk is a cadre of the state, you know, the twenty-fourth rank, with a salary of forty-three yuan a month. Besides, you have food and clothes free and don't have to stay here at night. You can even marry a woman if you want, and have your own home in a nearby village. Not a bad deal at all. Things have changed these days. We plan to receive many tourists, and the temple will be expanded. Anyway, I wish you good luck, young man."

"Wait a minute," Lu said. He put his sinewy hand on the opening and asked, "Do you know who I should talk to?"

"Your brigade leaders. You have to be elected by the commune members, I guess; or at least recommended by the Party branch. Good luck. I hope to see you here someday." The opening was closed and the light disappeared.

As though struck by a thunderbolt, Lu dropped onto the stone steps and remained blank for a few minutes. Then he jumped to his feet, picked up the bundle, and was about to run back.

No, he changed his mind, I can't leave like this. The goddamn monk is sleeping inside while keeping me outside in the dank night. No, this is not equal. This is not socialism. I must leave him some work to do. Lu unbuckled his belt, pulled down his pants, and hunkered down, emptying his bowels right in front of the gate. After a few relieving moans, he fished for paper in his pockets, but couldn't find any. Luckily, there was a piece of cornstalk lying on a step; he picked it up and cleaned himself with three strokes. He stood up and threw the stalk over the wall. "Keep it, you fat seedless monk," he barked.

Even having left the pile of fresh excrement couldn't cool him off. On his way back he swore continuously. Damn it, if you've bad luck, even a fart can sprain your back. Screw every one of them, including all the new monks. Someday I'll ride the Wheel of Wind and Fire through the sky and burn down every home of those bastards. I'll begin with Chu's hut and stable. Burning, burning, burning, burn up every blade of grass!

When he arrived home the heavy dew of the small hours soaked him through. His teeth were chattering as he lit the lamp with a trembling hand. To his surprise, the note was no longer on the table. Holding the lamp, he searched about but couldn't find it. Then he went into the kitchen and found the note lying on the floor. It must have been a wind that brought it here, he thought. No, what if it wasn't the wind? What if those bastards have read it?

His hair stood up, and a mist rose before his eyes for a minute or two. He sat down on the bed, holding the corner of the dining table, shook his head, and sighed. He tried to collect his thoughts. Whether they've read this or not, I mustn't stay. If they know of my trip to the temple and get hold of me, there'll be a denunciation meeting tomorrow. My crime is doubled now. There's no chance for clemency anymore. I must go, go far away.

But where can I go? To Uncle's home in Green Village? No, that'll get him into trouble. How about going into the Great Emperor Mountain for a while? But there are wolves and tigers in the forest. Too dangerous.

Then the idea of begging came to his mind. Yes, that's it. I'll go begging around. No, not "around." I'm going to big cities, to Beijing and Shanghai. They say lots of beggars have gotten rich and carry thousands of yuan in their belts; they live in hotels at night, and only during the day do they beg in the streets. Yes, I'll go to Beijing first. A wise man must read ten thousand volumes and travel ten thousand kilometers. Since I'm still young, it's time to see the world and learn about our motherland and folkways. In Beijing, I'll see all the palaces, the museums, the historic sites, and Tiananmen Square, the largest one in the world. It's too bad that Chairman Mao doesn't inspect Red Guards anymore, or I'd see his glorious face and his stalwart body on the gate tower as well.

How about Fulan and Leopard? I can't worry so much. They won't starve at home, will they? She can get everything from her parents. Once I have money, I'll buy her a diamond watch. She'll love it and look at it day and night with a broad smile. Then she'll forget what I've done. Money and wealth can always turn a woman's head.

"Today I feel unhappy at home, so I'm leaving for the capital," he chanted rather cheerfully. But someday I'll come back as a big official, whip every one of those leaders, and make them all kneel on the ground begging me for mercy. I'll forgive none of them and have them all beheaded, even though they want to pay me a large ransom.

He thought of writing a short letter, but changed his mind and placed the lamp on the old note. Let them go to the temple to get me, he said to himself. By then, I'll already have flown high and far.

Once he was outside the house, a constriction rose in his chest and tears came to his eyes. Revenge, he told himself. Someday I'll wipe out all their clans and wash their homes in a sea of blood. With the bundle on his back he turned around and walked into the pale dawn.

After two hours' journey he arrived at Dismount Fort. He went directly to the train station, but he didn't buy a ticket. From now on, he had to learn to get whatever he wanted without paying a fen. Four beggars were sleeping in a corner inside the hall. Having hesitated for a few seconds, Lu went to join them, lying supine on the cement floor. With the bundle under his head and his army cap covering his face, he soon fell asleep. Though footsteps tapped about and clanking trains passed by, Lu was so tired that nothing disturbed him.

When he woke up, it was already past three in the afternoon. All the beggars were gone except an old man with red-rimmed eyes sitting against the wall and holding an empty bottle in his lap. A locomotive was blowing its steam horn outside. Inside the dim hall a few rectangular patches of sunlight stretched on the floor. Lu's stomach rumbled and he felt hungry, but first he had to find out how to get to Beijing.

He asked the old beggar about the train schedule, but was surprised to learn that there was no train bound for the capital. The old man said Lu had better sneak onto the midnight freight train to Dalian first. Lu was a little confused by the advice. Then he realized that if he took a passenger train without a ticket, the attendants and the police could easily find him out and kick him off at any station.

After clarifying that, he got up and went out to solve the problem of hunger. Not knowing where to look for food, he walked along Market Street heading downtown. In front of Four Sea Fish Shop were about a hundred people lining up to buy something. Lu was curious and walked over. Seeing mountains of clams and oysters on the mat-covered ground, he felt his mouth watering. The folks here have a good life, he thought. They can have seafood every day. If only I could eat a few oysters. Oh, I'm so hungry. I'd like to bite them with the shells on.

But he tore himself away and took a right turn into Bath Street. The smell of fried leeks was hovering in the air. He caught the aroma and followed it instinctively. After he passed New Life Medical-Herb Store, the sign of Victory Restaurant emerged on the right. Lu hastened his steps to the door. He pushed aside the curtain made of glass beads and entered the restaurant. About twenty diners were inside, but two teenage beggars were already sitting in a corner waiting for leftovers. Lu went to sit beside them and wanted to see how they begged.

A moment later one of the boys got up and walked to a nearby table, where a fat middle-aged man was eating with a small girl, obviously his daughter. Without saying a word the boy held out his hand beside the steaming dishes. The fat man broke his bread and put a piece on the dirty hand. Immediately the other beggar went up to the table and got his share. Lu followed suit and received a chunk of bread too. "All right, no more," the fat man said, and waved to Lu to go away.

Lu had never thought getting food could be so easy. Just stretch out you hand and you'll have white, tender, fresh bread to eat. It tasted so good that he thought he had never eaten steamed bread so delicious.

Then a young waitress with slanting eyes came by, carrying a large fried yellow croaker still sizzling in the plate. After putting the dish in front of an old man, she pointed at the three beggars and said, "You stay there and wait until the customers finish, or you get out of here." Strange to say, her menacing words sounded to Lu like a sweet tune. What a goddess! he thought.

Three other women, in their thirties and forties, were also busy waiting tables, but this young woman was absolutely glamorous in Lu's eyes. Her skin was whiter than the bread just out of the steamer. He looked at her fingers, so exquisite and almost transparent. And those gorgeous glossy bangs. She ought to be tender and pretty, Lu thought; see what they eat here, all the delicacies from sea and land. Feeding on such food, even a pig would grow smooth and sleek.

Within two hours, Lu was stuffed with jelly soup, fried tofu, fish, oysters, pork, cabbages, pies, noodles, and even a half cup of sorghum liquor. Never at one meal had he eaten so many good things, which made him feel as if he were celebrating the Spring Festival. But something seemed missing. Yes, that young beauty. If only he could get close to her and pinch that pair of white paws. That would be real fun.

Unfortunately, a banquet was served after eight, so the three beggars were turned out. Having no place to go, Lu returned to the train station. The alcohol made him dizzy, yet he was very happy, because he found a beggar's life more enjoyable than his life at Ox Village. I ate so many good things, he thought, without paying a fen or raising a finger for them. Wonderful. I should stay here for some days, to eat more good stuff. If lucky, I can make a pass at that charming wench. Pretty, so pretty. He made clicks with his tongue, which wiped his lips now and then.

But another voice rose within him: You've forgotten all the trouble, huh? Bewitched by your lust for women again? Shame. Your wound hasn't begun to heal yet, but you've begun to forget the pain.

He looked down at his crotch. You little devil of a penis, you're playing tricks on me again. You can't take me in this time. I must go, go to Dalian tonight and switch trains there for Beijing. Too much pleasure surely weakens a man's will. I mustn't indulge myself. I've a long way to travel, to pursue a future of ten thousand kilometers. Besides, it's always better on the road than at an inn.

He lay on the floor, taking catnaps and waiting for the midnight freight train. At ten o'clock he was roused by voices shouting, "Wake up! Wake up!"

Three militiamen were pushing with their feet the beggars sleeping in the hall. Each of them wore a long wooden club across his back. "Show me your identification," a short militiaman said to the man lying beside Lu.

The beggar put his hand into a pocket inside his jacket and took out a piece of paper. The militiaman read it carefully and gave it back to him. Then he pointed at Lu and demanded, "Your identification."

"What identification?" Lu didn't understand what was going on.

"The paper that allows you to beg around."

"Where can I get it?" Lu blurted out.

"From your brigade. Do you have it or not?"

"I had it yesterday, but I've lost it somewhere. I can't find it. Sorry."

The militiaman screwed up his brows. "Lost it? Who can believe you? You didn't even know where to get it. I think you are an escaped counterrevolutionary. If you can't prove who you are, you must come with us."

Lu knew it was no use refusing, so he got to his feet, standing by respectfully. After going through all the beggars, the militia took him to the police station on Old Folk Road. The policeman on duty told him that if he refused to identify himself, they would commit him to a reform-through-labor team. Lu was terrified, because he remembered that a "troublemaker" in his village had been sent to a place like that by the brigade leaders and had died of dysentery there two months later. Without any delay he confessed who he was and where he came from. They telephoned Ox Village and were told that Lu was being examined, and that they should send him back as soon as possible.

"I could tell at first sight that he was a bad egg," the short militiaman said. He went up to Lu and removed the fountain pen from his breast pocket. "You don't need this. Pretending you can write, hmm? How many bottles of ink have you drunk?" He dropped the pen into a drawer.

Lu trembled all over, fearing they would search him. He had eleven yuan in his trouser pocket and two packets of expensive cigarettes in the bundle. Luckily, they didn't bother to look further.

That very night a jeep was going to Sand County to bring back the police chief, so they put Lu into the jeep, gave the driver a Russian 1951 pistol, and told him to drop Lu at Ox Village on the way. "If he escapes, shoot him," the policeman said loudly to the driver.

Lu had never been in an automobile; though he felt rather excited seeing houses, lights, trees, and wire poles flitting past, he was too anxious to enjoy the ride. He dared not move his body in the jeep, and kept wondering what was waiting for him in the village.

It was past midnight when he was back in his house again. After lighting the lamp, he was surprised to find nothing seemed to have changed. Even the note was still under the lamp. He picked it up and saw, beneath his own writing, four big characters: "Nets Above, Snares Below." It was Secretary Zhao's handwriting.

Oh, Lu thought with a moan, it's impossible to go anywhere. I can't escape. They'll never leave me alone until I write out what they want. All the officials are of one family; I can never jump out of their palms.

After burning the note over the lamp, he lit a joss stick to keep mosquitoes away. Tired of worrying, he remembered an old saying: "If the enemy come, we have troops to stop them; if a flood comes, we have earth to dam it." Worrying is useless, he told himself; the cart will find its way around the hill when it gets there. He took off his clothes and went to bed, allowing himself not to think of anything. Soon he fell asleep.

He snored for seven hours without a stop. When he woke up, the sun already covered half the bed. He stretched his legs in the sunlight and began worrying about the confession and thinking how to avoid the trial in the evening. Unable to come up with a plausible excuse and unable to stop missing the slant-eyed waitress, he resumed cursing himself. All the trouble came from his inability to control his penis. Strange to say, that little fellow, ignoring its master's disgust and hatred, went erect again, bulging the front of the underwear like a torpedo. Lu hated it. If only he could have plucked it out! It had no shame and fear, and wanted to go into action even in the face of danger and annihilation. He got up and put on his clothes. Still the erection wouldn't go away. He gave it two slaps with the sole of his rubber shoe. The beating somehow scared the little devil down.

Lu went out, washed his face, took a corn cake, and hurried to the field with a hoe on his shoulder and a large straw hat on his head. Whatever had happened, he must not be slack in his work. He should pretend that everything was normal.

Evening came. With only five pages of writing and with the vision of the leaders furious at his attempted escape, Lu dared not go to the brigade's office. He thought it better to stay home and wait until the leaders' anger waned a little. If they asked him the next day, he would say he had a stomachache and couldn't walk, and would beg them for a few more days. He cooked himself a pot of noodles with string beans, but he was too worried to enjoy the food; he forced himself to think how to make a few more passages of the confession.

The clock with a long pendulum ticked away on the red chest. In the room two ducks perched in a corner while a few chickens strutted and pecked about. On the broad brick bed were scattered his son's clothes and toys and his wife's sewing bowl, filled with scraps of cloth, threads, partly stitched soles, scissors, awls. It was stuffy, so after supper Lu took off his undershirt and pants, wearing only the shorts. He sat by the scrawled sheets of paper absentmindedly.

He didn't expect the leaders would come to his home to look for him. The second he saw them in the yard, he lay down and held his stomach with both hands. They burst in, and Wang yelled at him, "Sit up, you son of a tortoise!"

"Oh, I'm sick."

"Don't play tricks with your grandpas. We can see through you. Get up. I saw you hoeing turnips two hours ago. No illness can be so quick. Get your damn ass up!"

Without a word Lu climbed up and sat on the edge of the bed.

"Why do you try to trick us?" Secretary Zhao questioned.

"I'm sick. I really can't walk."

"Cut it out," Wang bellowed. "We know how you feel." Then he lowered his voice. "All right, we're going to take care of our patient tonight. Come with us. We'll cure you of your illness in a couple of days."

Lu was terrified, his scalp numb. He knew they would apply the tactics called "cartwheeling"—they would take turns questioning him day and night, not allowing him to sleep until he collapsed, confessed everything, even invented things to please them. He could not possibly resist so many of them. If necessary, the leaders could send for a platoon of militiamen. He was so scared that he broke into tears. "Oh, I've cracked my brains, but can't write more. I really don't know how to write. I've used a bottle of ink already. Please let me go just this once. I'm going to kowtow to you."

"Hold it," Wang ordered. "You can't deceive us any longer."

Scribe Hsiao stepped forward and restrained Lu from going to his knees.

"Oh, heaven," Lu cried out, "how can I convince you of my sincerity? Do you want me to die? All right—my family's already broken, and I don't want to live anymore." He pulled a pair of large scissors out of the sewing bowl and put them against his throat. "No more! If you want my life, say it. I'll die here to show you my remorse."

"Stop bluffing," Wang said, smiling with contempt. "I know what stuff'll come out the moment you raise your buttocks. Do it, kill yourself. Then we'll believe you're a good, progressive comrade."

"Lu Han, don't take us to be beardless idiots," Zhao said. "Who's ever heard that a man killed himself with scissors. That's woman stuff."

"Do it," Wang ordered. "Let's have an eye-opener. We'll name you a Revolutionary Martyr and give your family provisions."

Lu was wailing, tears rolling down his cheeks.

"Yes, do it," Zhao demanded with his arms open. "We're waiting. If you don't, you're not a Chinese."

Lu moved down the scissors as if to prove his inability to kill himself. He turned around and bent down.

"What are you doing?" Wang said.

Lu ripped open his shorts, pulled out his scrotum, and cut it off together with the testicles. He dropped the cutting and fell to the ground, screaming and groaning. Immediately the chickens rushed over and carried away those meaty parts.

"Stop the chickens and get his balls back!" Wang yelled, kicking at a duck that was on its way to the bloody spot.

Both the secretary and the scribe ran out, but it was too late—the chickens had disappeared into the dark yard. Inside, Wang was busy stanching the bleeding with a towel. The sleeves of his white shirt were covered with bloodstains. Still Wang never stopped cursing. "Damn your ancestors. Who told you to do this? I hope you're bleeding to death."

"I hate it, hate it!" Lu said through his teeth, clenched to choke his moaning. One of his legs was twitching, the toe drawing small circles on the ground.

Finally Wang managed to tie up Lu's crotch with three towels, and the blood was almost stopped. Then Hsiao returned with several men and with Chu's horse cart. They wrapped Lu up with a flowery quilt and carried him out. The moment they placed him in the cart, the horses set out galloping to the Commune Clinic in Dismount Fort. Both the leaders went with the cart. They even gave Lu sweet-potato liquor on the way to stop him from moaning and shaking.

Lu's self-castration earned him freedom. Nobody thought of pressing him for the confession again, since his act had indeed proved his remorse and sincerity. Naturally, a lot of men shook hands with him when he was back from town. The leaders even went to his father-in-law's house the day after the castration and tried to persuade Lu's wife to forgive him and come back home. On hearing of the sad news, Fulan burst into tears, saying she was guilty and shouldn't have mistreated her husband that way. Her father, a well-respected old man, scolded her in front of the leaders and ordered her to go back at once. That very day she returned with Baby Leopard in Chu's horse cart. Now she wanted to take good care of Lu and was determined to be a model wife.

As for Lu, he felt things were fine. Losing his testicles didn't differ much from being sterilized by the family-planning team. Quite a few men in the village were emasculated that way, and the only difference was that they carried more weight below their bellies. Let others babble whatever they liked. Yes, he was gelded, but he had a son, who was as strong as a bear cub, to carry on his family line. From now on that devil of a penis would cause no trouble, and his family would enjoy peace and unity, which would surely lead to security and prosperity. Though he sweated more than before while working in the fields, he felt his back never so straight and his body never so sturdy. People noticed his face glowing with ruddy health and his hair turning darker and thicker. He did so well that the villagers elected him an exemplary commune member. Secretary Zhao even had a heart-to-heart talk with him and encouraged him to write an application for Party membership, which Lu was, of course, delighted to do. Most significant of all, he had a new, normal life.

■ A Decade

I left the countryside twelve years ago when my father was transferred to an artillery division in Dalian. Ever since then we have
lived in the city. If my aunt were not in Dismount Fort, I might
have forgotten that small town where I went to elementary school
only for two years in the late 1960s. My aunt comes to visit us
every fall, helping Mother prepare our winter clothes and pickle
vegetables. Once in a while she brings that town back to my
memory.

Last summer I went to Dismount Fort for the first time after
a decade. The town was smaller than I had thought. Every street
seemed shorter than it had been. On the first day, I rode my
uncle's Peacock bicycle to the marketplace, the Blue Brook, the
Eastern Bridge, White Mansion—our classroom building, and
other places that I still remembered. But the distances between
them were so short I visited them all in less than two hours.
From the second day on I gave up the bicycle, and instead I
walked around. Few people knew me, because my family had
never lived in the town and I had stayed at my aunt's when going to school there. After strolling through the streets, I found
the town basically the same, and the only difference was that

there were fewer children now. I stopped at some houses where my former classmates had lived, but they had all left, working in nearby counties and cities. Most girls had become textile workers in Gold County. Their parents didn't remember me. There was only one boy who had not left and whose mother still knew me, but he was jailed for raping two women.

Life in the countryside was dull. There was nothing going on in the evenings. After supper most people would sit outside, chatting away and fanning themselves until the cool breeze came from the Yellow Sea around midnight. I missed my boyfriend, who was my classmate at the college. He stayed with his parents in Tianjin during the summer. At night I would write to him. If tired of writing, I read Turgenev's *Smoke* and a current issue of *Youth*, a small literary magazine published in Shenyang, which carried a story of mine. Since I had time, I read the whole issue from cover to cover. I didn't like most of the pieces in it, but there was a narrative poem that aroused my interest. The poem tells a story from a former Red Guard's point of view. At the beginning of the Cultural Revolution a teenage boy together with his classmates paraded their teacher, an old man, through the streets. The boy kicked the teacher hard and broke his ribs. For the following years he was full of remorse and tried to make up for what he had done. Then the teacher fell ill, and the boy, a young man now, looked after him for five months until the old man died with gratitude. I didn't like the sentiment of the poem, but it reminded me of a young woman teacher, Zhu Wenli, who had taught me at the Central Elementary School in Dismount Fort eleven years before.

I was in the fourth grade when she came to our school. At a glance you could tell she was a recent college graduate. She looked shy and timid. In the beginning, whenever she spoke, not only her cheeks but also her ears turned red. She was a charming young woman, tall and slender, her hands very delicate with long, thin fingers. Her dark eyes were as sensitive as though they were always ready to be in tears. At that time, in the middle of the revolution, we had no sense of beauty. As one of the slogans says: "Sweet flowers are poisonous." To us, Wenli was someone dangerous rather than pretty. But I remember I liked looking at her in profile; in that way she reminded me of the ballerinas in the revolutionary model play *The Red Women Detachment.* Certainly Wenli never wore a uniform; besides, her lips were thicker and the tip of her small nose too round, lacking the stern looks of a woman soldier.

She taught music in her first year. The class mainly consisted of two parts: the songs praising Chairman Mao or composed for the quotations from him; the dances expressing our loyalty to the Chairman and the Party. Though she was knowledgeable about music and was even able to compose a song, Wenli's voice was much too soft and too weak for those revolutionary songs. We believed we sang better than she, because our voices were more sincere and passionate. But she was a wonderful dancer. Standing on one toe, she could raise the other leg slowly back and forth with ease, as if it had no weight. She could stretch out her arms with a lot of grace and poise. We all enjoyed watching her dance, though she didn't seem to have the strength for a loyalty dance, the vigorous kind we did on the streets. Soon we learned that she came from a capitalist family in Shanghai. No wonder she looked so delicate and fragile.

One day at noon, Niu Fen and I went to see Miao Jian, the teacher in charge of our class, whose office was on the second floor in White Mansion. On the last flight of the stairs we heard someone singing. The slow, dangling tune was so different from anything we had heard that both of us stopped to listen. It was Wenli's voice. Gradually we took in the words:

> Why are flowers so red?
> So red and so beautiful?
> O so red, O so beautiful,
> Like a fire,
> Like a fire
> That burns the blood
> Of youth and love—

The wind must have blown open the door of her office. She stopped. Niu Fen and I entered the corridor and found Wenli holding the doorknob. She saw us and smiled nervously, her lips twitching slightly and her eyes full of sparkling tears.

"Can I help you, Aina?" she asked me. I shook my head, too confused by her tearful eyes to say anything. One of my bobby pins came loose and I stuck it back in my hair.

"What's that song, Teacher Zhu?" Niu Fen, who was a loud-mouth, asked.

"A Uigur folk song," Wenli said. "I, I sang it just for fun."

I don't know whether Niu Fen reported Wenli to the school leaders. After that, I never heard her sing the song again, and she only sang the revolutionary songs she taught us in class. But somehow the tune of that folk song remained in my mind; from time to time it rose in my ears. Later I came upon its music and words at a friend's home in Dalian and learned to sing it myself.

Our class teacher Maio Jian was a young man. Some people called him "Little Albanian," because of his big round eyes, aquiline nose, and small stature. In no way did he look Chinese.

His face was very lean and he had to shave every day to keep his whiskers down. It was said that he had mixed blood. People thought him handsome, perhaps because he looked exotic. I had no idea when he and Wenli started their love affair. In any case, we soon noticed they were often together. Later Wenli had appendicitis and was operated upon. During her recovery Miao visited her every day.

One afternoon in the fall Niu Fen, Zhang Wei, and I went to Miao's office to get some pamphlets for the class. On his door hung a sign, "No Admittance," which had never been there before. We were uncertain if he was in, but we heard a noise inside. The three of us pressed our eyes on the cracks of the door to see what was going on. Both Miao and Wenli were standing by the window, but Wenli, her hips leaning against a desk, was unbuckling her belt.

"Just let me have a peek," Miao said softly.

Outside we three looked at each other and stuck our tongues out. Then we heard Wenli say, "Just a peek, promise?"

"I promise."

She pulled down her pants a little and revealed her white belly. "Lower, lower," Miao urged.

The pants went down further, and a scar like a caterpillar, about three inches long, appeared close to her right groin. Miao touched the dark skin with his index finger, then bent down and kissed the scar. "Naughty, you're a naughty boy," Wenli said happily and pulled up her pants.

Bewildered by what we witnessed, the three of us turned around simultaneously and dashed to the head of the stairs as though escaping provoked hornets. Our footsteps must have startled them, for I heard Miao cry, "Oh heaven!"

Either Niu Fen or Zhang Wei told on them. Next morning we were summoned to the office of the school's Revolutionary Committee. The leaders asked us to describe what we had seen and heard; without hesitation we told them all the details. We thought our teachers had done something bad and shameful, but we had no idea how serious it was. Director Liu said the two teachers were corrupt to the bones by bourgeois lifestyle.

In three days our school was covered with big-character posters exposing and condemning Miao Jian and Zhu Wenli. Many articles appeared on the walls and billboards, such as "Root Out the Bourgeois Lifestyle," "It's Shameless to Open Your Pants in the Office," "Why Do You Still Behave like a Hoodlum?" "Zhu Wenli: the Stinking Bourgeois Miss," "New China Does Not Tolerate the Incorrigible Progeny of Capitalists." In the music class two days later, Wenli looked very pale, her eyes swollen and her voice a little hoarse. She tried to teach a song that expressed the Tibetans' love for Chairman Mao, but we weren't very interested. Quite a few students made faces at each other. Two boys even buckled and unbuckled their belts with meaningful noise.

Then Miao was sent to the country to be reformed through labor in the fields. Wenli was assigned to take over our class. She didn't teach music anymore, because one of the school leaders had complained that she sounded as though wailing when singing a song which should be full of gusto, in accordance with the courageous spirit of the proletariat. Most students in our class were children of poor peasants, workers, and cadres, so it was not easy for Wenli to teach us. But unlike the boys, who often made insinuating remarks about her family background or imitated her voice, a number of girls were good to her, because they liked the way she danced and wanted her to teach them how to dance. Since I was clumsy, not cut out for dancing, I was never close to her. I noticed she seldom spoke to anyone outside class. A few wrinkles, very thin, appeared at the ends of her eyes. Her hair was no longer as tidy as before.

After the Spring Festival we began to study a new lesson in our Chinese class. The text was a letter Chairman Mao had written to the Albanian Communist Party. As usual, Wenli led us to read it out three times, and then she started to explain the new words and expressions. In the letter, there was a sentence that went like this: "You (the Albanian Communist Party) are a grand eagle soaring bravely; in comparison, the Russian Revisionists and the American Imperialists are merely a pile of yellowish dirt."

Wenli said to the class, "Chairman Mao here uses a metaphor. Who knows what a metaphor is?"

We had never heard of that word, so nobody responded. Wenli wrote out the word on the blackboard and went on, "A metaphor is to compare one thing to something else. For example . . . " she coughed into her fist, "the Russian Revisionists and the American Imperialists are not dirt, but Chairman Mao describes them as dirt. That's a metaphor."

"I have a question, teacher," Gao Jiang said and stood up. He was the tallest boy in the class.

"What's your question?" Wenli asked with a start.

"You say the Russian Revisionists and the American Imperialists are not dirt, but Chairman Mao says clearly they are dirt. Why?"

Wenli's lips were quivering, but she managed to say, "They aren't dirt. They are also people like us. We call them dirt merely to show our contempt for them."

"You mean they are also humans?" Niu Fen challenged.

"Ye-yes," Wenli said.

The class was in a tumult now. Many of us were convinced that Wenli was wrong, not only wrong but reactionary. How dare she change Chairman Mao's meaning! How could we trust such a teacher? Like her capitalist father, she must have hated our socialist country and our great Party all the time.

Wenli was so frightened she called off the class ten minutes before recess. Then some of us went straight to the Workers' Propaganda Team, which consisted of five illiterate men from the Food Company, to report her. After hearing us, the vice-director, Li Long, slapped his copy of Chairman Mao's quotations on the desk and said, "Damn her grandmother, that bitch will never change. Now she's done enough."

The next day we had a new teacher. In a week Wenli was sent to the countryside. I don't know to what village. At that time I didn't care where she went; wherever she was sent, it seemed to me that she deserved it. Besides, there were so many people being reformed through labor that Wenli's leaving was almost a natural thing.

The image of Wenli came to mind time and again, so I decided to visit her before I left, if she was still in Dismount Fort. Not because I wanted to apologize; I hadn't done anything on purpose to hurt her. Though I didn't know what to say to her exactly, my visit would at least assure her that a student of hers had not forgotten her after a decade.

One evening I asked Aunt and Uncle about her. "Wenli, you mean?" Aunt said with a big smile, her face full of creases and puckers. "She's different now. She's a strong woman in town. Everybody knows her."

"Is she still a teacher in the elementary school?"

"No, she doesn't teach anymore. You know, after the government canceled all the class-status stuff, she was back from the country and became a free person like us. Now she's the vice-president of the elementary school."

"Is she married?"

"Of course. She has two kids, a boy and a girl, nice kids."

"Who's her husband? Miao Jian?"

"I don't know. He's also a cadre or something. My old man," Aunt touched Uncle with her palm-leaf fan, "do you know who is Wenli's husband? His name?"

"You bet I know. He's Wang Dadong, the director of the People's Bank in town."

Uncle told me Miao Jian had left the country for Hong Kong seven years before. It was said that his granduncle was a rich, childless merchant, so Miao went there to inherit the wealth. Anyway, it seemed nothing had happened between him and Wenli. Aunt said Wenli's family now lived in the granite house at the corner of East and Safe streets. I remembered that house well, where my classmate Dongdong had once lived.

The conversation with Aunt and Uncle made me more determined to see Wenli. The next afternoon I asked Aunt what gift I should take to Wenli if I paid her a visit.

"That's easy, go buy two packets of walnut cookies," she said.

I felt uneasy about that. Wenli used to be my teacher, a graceful delicate woman; cookies would show I had no taste. Unlike the country people who were obsessed with good food, Wenli had never seemed to be interested in eating. I had a new pink skirt with me, but I didn't know her size now; she must have been much taller than I. Having thought it over, I decided to take the issue of *Youth* as a gift, since it contained a story of mine, which would probably convince her that I, as a student of hers once, had been trying to live up to some of the expectations that she might have cherished for herself in the past. I would tell her that I wanted to be a writer—a novelist and playwright—even though I couldn't dance well.

After dinner I set out for East Street, which was just about three hundred paces away. In the dusk a half-moon was wavering beyond the water tower and the buildings within the army compound. Here and there chimneys were puffing out bands of smoke, which were dangling in the indigo sky. The street was much quieter than ten years before. I remembered playing soldier here with boys and girls at dusk, shouting and throwing cabbage roots and rotten turnips at each other.

The moment I entered East Street a small crowd appeared ahead on the left side. I heard people quarreling and calling each other names. Their sharp voices, male and female, fluctuated through the air like sounds sent over by a tweeter from a long distance. I walked closer and saw men and women arguing and gesticulating under a road lamp.

"No, that's not true! Your chicken never came into our yard to lay an egg," a stalwart woman in white pajamas said loudly, waving a rolling pin.

"I saw it enter your yard this afternoon, and I heard it clucking afterwards," a small woman said, holding a white hen in her arms.

"Liar! Why didn't you come and pick it up then?"

Two men, who were apparently the husbands, tried to stop the women, saying it was merely an egg, not worth it.

"No," the small woman said to her husband, "it's not just an egg. Look at that shrew, she can kill me if I come near her." Then she turned to the tall woman. "Zhu Wenli, you're a cadre and have drunk a lot of ink. I'm just a housewife and don't read books. I don't care if we scratch each other's faces."

"If you dare to touch me, I'll break your skull with this," the stalwart woman said, sucking her teeth, and raised the rolling pin. She spat to the ground.

I looked closely. She was indeed my teacher Zhu Wenli, but her thick body and fleshy face belied the young person I had known. A pale scar under her nostrils tightened the upper lip and made her mouth protrude a little. All the tenderness and innocence which had marked that face was now replaced by a numb, stony look. Even her voice had changed too, full of scratchy metal. If the small woman hadn't mentioned her name, I would never have been able to recognize her. Indeed she looked very strong, as Aunt had told me, but she was no longer the person I wanted to meet. Somehow I was overwhelmed by a kind of hatred rising in me.

Her husband, a short balding man, held her arm, turned her around, and pulled her away. Together they were returning to the granite house. A feeling of misery filled my chest, similar to how I had felt when my first boyfriend left me for another girl. Things turned misty before my eyes, and I found myself in tears.

HA JIN is the author of two books of poetry and another short story collection, *Ocean of Words*, winner of the 1997 PEN/ Hemingway Award for Fiction. He has received many other writing awards, including three Pushcart Prizes for his short stories and the *Kenyon Review* Prize for Fiction. He teaches at Emory University.

The Flannery O'Connor Award for Short Fiction

David Walton, *Evening Out*

Leigh Allison Wilson, *From the Bottom Up*

Sandra Thompson, *Close-Ups*

Susan Neville, *The Invention of Flight*

Mary Hood, *How Far She Went*

François Camoin, *Why Men Are Afraid of Women*

Molly Giles, *Rough Translations*

Daniel Curley, *Living with Snakes*

Peter Meinke, *The Piano Tuner*

Tony Ardizzone, *The Evening News*

Salvatore La Puma, *The Boys of Bensonhurst*

Melissa Pritchard, *Spirit Seizures*

Philip F. Deaver, *Silent Retreats*

Gail Galloway Adams, *The Purchase of Order*

Carole L. Glickfeld, *Useful Gifts*

Antonya Nelson, *The Expendables*

Nancy Zafris, *The People I Know*

Debra Monroe, *The Source of Trouble*

Robert H. Abel, *Ghost Traps*

T. M. McNally, *Low Flying Aircraft*

Alfred DePew, *The Melancholy of Departure*

Dennis Hathaway, *The Consequences of Desire*

Rita Ciresi, *Mother Rocket*

Dianne Nelson, *A Brief History of Male Nudes in America*

Christopher McIlroy, *All My Relations*

Alyce Miller, *The Nature of Longing*

Carol Lee Lorenzo, *Nervous Dancer*

C. M. Mayo, *Sky Over El Nido*

Wendy Brenner, *Large Animals in Everyday Life*

Paul Rawlins, *No Lie Like Love*

Harvey Grossinger, *The Quarry*

Ha Jin, *Under the Red Flag*